MW01489632

This book is a work imagination. All names, characters, events, places, products etc. have been used for this fictional purpose. If, by chance, they or it resembles someone or something; living or dead, it is by coincidence. All scriptures are taken from the Bible and is not the work of the author.

Published by: Twins Write 2 Publishing
© 2022 by Lakisha Johnson
All rights reserved

Almost Destroyed 2

Will the light be enough?

dedication

This book is dedicated to the woman or man whose been almost destroyed by the strains and struggle of life but has survived.

Thank you for getting up and trying again.

gratitude

I'll always begin by thanking God. It's Him who believes enough in who He created to trust me with this gift. This is why, even when its hard and doesn't pay off like I expect, I'll never give up. Each day, I accept this gift, proudly and unapologetically serving God through the pages of a fiction book.

To my entire family, know I love each of you for supporting me, release after release.

To my sister Laquisha and my girl, Shakendria ... thank you for always being willing to help me on this tedious journey.

To each of you who support Lakisha, the PreacHER, Author and Blogger ... THANK YOU! I wouldn't be who I am without you who purchase, download, recommend and review my books. Please, don't stop believing in me. We're connected now and that makes us family.

disclaimer

Ava's story is one of abuse, anger, and pain as she takes this journey of healing. Reading her story may trigger unresolved emotions and pain for you. Guard yourself and your heart. If this means you are unable to read this, I understand and pray one of my other books will be a better fit.

Here's the link to my website.

www.authorlakishajohnson.com

Also, this is a work of Christian Fiction and within this book is prayers, scriptures, sermons, and a whole lot of God. There's also cursing. Someone may ask, why the need to use foul language? I'll tell you. We're dealing with imperfect people and the raw emotions of anger. If these are the kinds of things you don't like to read and will cause you to leave a low review, I implore you to return this book.

For me, this isn't simply writing, it's ministry and sometimes ministry isn't confined to tradition. Yes, I get its Christian Fiction and most desire it to be "clean," but sometimes, we have to meet people where they are and unfortunately, it may be a place of darkness and pain.

Nonetheless, if you're deciding to read on, HAPPY READING and I hope you enjoy it. – Lakisha

Almost Destroyed
2

Will the light be enough?

chapter one

Once service is over, I meet everyone in the vestibule where I give each of them a hug before we head for brunch. June made reservations at a restaurant called Biscuits & Jam.

"I'm going by the bathroom then I'll meet y'all at the car." I tell them.

"I hope the food is good. I'm starving." I say to Katrina as we go into the stalls.

"Girl, me too. I skipped breakfast." A few seconds later, I hear her talking. "Yes. Hey. No, we're headed to brunch but let me call you right back. Yeah, I answered through my Air Pod. Okay. Bye silly."

"Bye silly." I joke.

"Oh hush." She laughs. "I'll wait for you outside." She washes her hands and goes out.

Coming out of the stall, I wash my hands. Opening the door, I walk up to see she's on Facetime. I move to pass her, freezing when I hear the voice.

"Why are you talking to my ex?" I angrily ask trying to snatch the phone.

She moves. "Your ex? What are you talking about?" she looks at the phone then back to me as June comes over.

"That's Andre."

"Wait, what's going on?" June inquires.

"She's on the phone with Andre."

"Andre? No, you're mistaken. His name is Donte. Babe, tell her."

He smirks then hangs up.

"Call him back."

She does, twice and he ignores the calls.

"Do you have any pictures?"

"Yeah." She fumbles with the phone. "See."

"Boo, his name is Andre Donte Powell, a Sagittarius, date of birth is December 12, 1977, shoe size is a thirteen but don't believe the hype, he used to be a police officer with no ambition and whatever he's sold you is a lie, a bold face lie. How did you meet him?"

"No. No." She repeats. "He must look like him or something. He told me his name was Donte who I met a few months ago at a Labor Day event—

"For the police department." I finish the sentence. "That's because his name is Andre and he's a liar."

"Oh my God, I feel sick. He's been lying to me this entire time."

"Katrina, please be honest. Did you know who he was?"

"No, I swear. Why don't you believe me?" she yells causing the few people left to turn around.

"What's going on?" the rest of the group rushes over.

"Katrina is dating Andre." June tells them. "Yet, I find it funny you didn't know who he was."

"I didn't." She asserts. "I've never met him nor seen a picture and he told me his name was Donte. I don't have a reason to lie."

"Ok, calm down and lower your tone. This is still a church." Larissa states.

"I can't believe this. Do you talk about me around him?" I ask.

"Yes, of course. You're my friend and he's my boyfriend. I didn't see anything wrong with talking about you."

"This isn't your fault." I assure her. "I'm willing to bet he knew who you were beforehand, and all of this is a way to get back at me. It's also how he knew so much about me. Katrina, I can't tell you what to do with your life, but Andre isn't it."

"She's being too nice." June cuts in. "Andre isn't worth the dog poop on the bottom of your shoe. You can do better. However, it's your life but you got to pick sis. It's either him or Ava."

"I can't." She says through tears. "Please don't make me choose."

When I see her grip her stomach, an angry chuckle escapes my lips. "Oh my God. You're pregnant."

"I recently found out and planned to tell him tonight. Ava, I'm sorry." She comes up to me.

"No." I insist. "Please go. I can't deal with this right now."

She swipes the tears from her face. "I didn't know who he was. I didn't, but please don't make me choose between my friend and the father of my child."

"Sweetie, no one is doing that, but as long as you're with him, you can't be around her." Naomi points to me.

"Nobody is talking to y'all. Please butt out." She screams. "Ava, can we go somewhere and talk?"

"This chick must be a donut short of a dozen." June states. "Cause who you yelling at Tricky Trina?"

"Okay everybody, take a breath and calm down." Josiah coaches. "Ma'am, we understand this wasn't your fault and we're sorry the both of you are having to deal with this. However, Ava has an order of protection against this man. How do you think she feels knowing you're sleeping with the person who tried to kill her?"

"How would I know when y'all won't let me talk to her?" She screams. "God."

"Whoa. What is going on?" Pastor Hunter rushes out with his wife behind him.

"I'm sorry Pastor and Lady Hunter." I reply to him. "I didn't mean to cause a scene. I found out something that upset me, and things got out of hand, but we're leaving."

"Not like this. Whatever has happened, let's try to resolve it. Will you all come talk to me?"

We follow him into a conference room.

"Katrina is dating Ava's ex. The same ex who tried to murder her not even two months ago and now she expects Ava to accept it." June tells him before he has a chance to ask again.

"That's not what I said. Stop putting words in my mouth." Katrina angrily responds.

"Somebody needs to since you aren't using the right ones, sis."

"I'm not your sis."

"Okay. Let's all take a breath." Pastor Hunter says.

"Pastor, I didn't know he was her ex when I met him *three* months ago. He's been lying to me too."

"If you met him on Labor Day, it hasn't been three months. Did you fail math in school?" June mocks and I touch her arm.

Katrina rolls her eyes. "Nevertheless, things are complicated. I'm pregnant."

"Well, you just met the Negro so you can't be but three days along." June mumbles.

"Stop picking apart everything I say. I know when we met and if you think I'm going to have an abortion, I won't, and neither will I keep this from him. Whatever happened between them has nothing to do with me. He isn't like what she described."

"That's easy for you to say after knowing him for 60 days." I tell her. "Even employees know how to act when on probation at a new job."

"Okay." Pastor Hunter intervenes. "If it's okay with everybody, may Lady Hunter and I have a moment with Katrina and Ava?"

"No need, she's already looking at me like I disgust her." Katrina states. "Ava, I get you're not okay with this, but he makes me happy and is the father of my child. He'll also never hurt me."

I chuckle. "Then have at him."

"I don't need your blessing. Have you stopped to think maybe things didn't work for y'all because you weren't the woman he needed?"

"Girl—you know what, you're right. I pray your woman enough to change him, so you'll never have to look into the eyes of the man you love while he wraps his hands around your throat so tight, your eyes burn. I pray you never have to spend weeks hiding behind closed doors while the black eyes, bruised ribs, and his fingerprints on your neck heal. I pray you'll never know what it feels like to be thrown out of his house like a diseased dog and all your property destroyed. I even pray you'll never know the sleepless nights, nightmares and panic attacks while recovering from a rape you replay in your subconscious because you were unconscious when he did it."

I grab my purse and walk to the door. "Oh, to be clear. This look isn't disgust, its pity knowing what's in store when you finally meet the real him. Here's a suggestion. Don't burn bridges. You'll need somebody when you he's drained you of everything. It just won't be me."

chapter two
Katrina

I watch Ava leave out of the room before sliding into a chair and putting my head in my hands.

"Katrina."

"Pastor Hunter, this isn't my fault, so please don't lecture me. How was I supposed to know he was her ex when he lied to me too? I truly thought he was who God sent. I mean, he checked all of the boxes."

"Checked all the boxes?" Lady Hunter asks confused.

I sigh. "He's everything I've been praying for. He's kind, handsome, attentive, got his own house, car, money, no baby momma drama, and he ain't on the down low. You know how rare he is? Why should I have to give him up because of his past with Ava? He hasn't hurt me, and we don't know for sure he hurt her. For all we know, she could be lying."

"So could he." Lady Hunter states. "Katrina, we aren't trying to convince you whether to stay or go. We simply want you to use sound wisdom and common sense. With everything you've learned today, do you think maybe this relationship is one of convenience and not love?"

"Please don't tell me you're taking her side?" I jump up from the chair. "I've been a member of this church for over seven years, and you'll believe someone you baptized this morning?"

"Katrina, calm down. There are no sides to take, yet you have to see where Ava is coming from." Pastor Hunter says.

"Ava sounds jealous if you ask me. A true friend would be happy for me."

"I can see you're not in a place to effectively hear sound advice, so let's plan to meet next week." He tells me.

"Wow." I chuckle. "Now I'm stupid and can't comprehend for wanting my child's father to be present in his or her life? Pastor Hunter, it sounds like you're the one who needs advice on how to properly counsel your sheep. Aren't we supposed to forgive people seventy times seven? Aren't we, as Christians, supposed to give grace? Why can't it be the same for Donte? He made one mistake."

"One that almost cost someone their life." His wife adds and I roll my eyes.

"What do y'all know?"

"Katrina, we're not here to make you feel bad. Our words, as hard as they are to hear, comes from a heartfelt place. Yet, you won't be able to receive them when your judgment is clouded by flesh. We don't want to see you hurt, however you're a grown woman who is capable of making her own decisions. We're going to pray your discernment allows you to see things for what they are in order to make the best decision for you and your baby's life."

"And we pray you're right about him and he can be all you need." Lady Hunter adds.

"Yeah well, y'all can save your prayers. I won't be back to this sham of a church."

I storm out. When I get to the car, I Facetime Donte again. He doesn't answer. I send a text telling him to meet me at my house.

Getting home, I pace in the living room waiting on him. An hour passes. I try calling him again, no answer. Four hours, no answer. I'm balled up in my bed when I hear the chirp of the alarm and him calling my name.

"Babe why are you in the dark?" he asks turning on the light.

"Who's asking, Donte or Andre?" I sit up wiping my face. "Why would you lie to me about who you are?"

"Technically I didn't lie. My middle name is Donte."

"It's still a lie when you're covering your true identity. I'm going to ask you this and you'd better be honest. Is being with me a way to get back at Ava?"

"No."

"Did you know who I was before we met?"

"No."

"Stop lying." I yell throwing a cell phone I found in his stuff. "I saw the screenshots of my Instagram feed."

"First, don't go through my stuff. Second, okay, yes. I saw the picture of you two on her Instagram and started following you. But, in my defense, meeting you at the BBQ was pure coincidence."

"Right. I bet it was." I chuckle. "The many times I've talked about my friend Ava, and you said nothing. Why not be honest with me?"

"And say what?" he gets loud. "Baby, your new friend is my ex who provoked me to an attack, lied like I raped her and now I might go to jail because of it." He mocks.

"Yes." I yell back. "Yes. You should have told me and given me the option to choose whether to be with you. Instead, I looked like a fool standing there listening to her say all the things you did to her in front of my Pastor. You said your ex was at fault for what happened to her, but I know Ava and she isn't like you described."

"Oh, so you have one conversation with her and now I'm the liar." He laughs. "After all we've had these past three months, you'll let Ava ruin it in what, ten minutes. Damn, do I mean nothing to you?"

"I didn't say that."

"If you want to break up, say it and I'll get my things, but I will not stand here while you tear me down. I told you I didn't do what she said. Yes, we had an argument and it got out of hand, but I never tried to kill her. Truth is, we were in the middle of making up when her landlord walked in on us."

"Did you rape her?"

"Hell no. Ava is a freak and liked having kinky sex. I admit I had my hand around her throat, but she begged me to do it. Then she saw him, was embarrassed and lied."

"What about the black eyes and bruised ribs?"

"Did you see her with a black eye? I mean, y'all were friends, right? If she had black eyes and bruised ribs, wouldn't you have known?"

"I didn't see her while she was healing. I never got any of her calls and voicemails."

"Right, and I guess I had something to do with that too. I'm telling you. She's lying and that's the God honest truth. I don't know why no one believes me." He chokes up. "I lost my job, on the verge of losing my house and now, you. Babe, I'll never intentionally hurt a woman with my hands." He sits on the side of the bed with his face covered. "It's like everybody is against me."

"Donte—Andre, baby stop." I crawl over to him. "I didn't say I believed her. I only want to know why you felt like you couldn't be truthful with me."

"I knew you'd think I was only here for some kind of revenge. Boo, meeting you at the BBQ was strictly chance and although I wasn't looking for a relationship, I started falling for you. You made me feel like a man again after Ava tried to strip me of my dignity. I'm sorry for not being honest, but I thought we'd hook up and be done. I never expected for us to fall in love."

"You love me?" I question raising his head.

"Why is it hard to believe? Haven't I shown you?" he pushes me away and stands.

"I'm sorry for accusing you. I was angry after being ganged up on by Ava and the get fresh crew and you wouldn't even answer the phone."

"I'm sorry. My phone died, but I came straight here once I got the chance and it's still not enough. Trina, I spent too many years in a relationship with a weak woman who couldn't be what I needed, and I won't make that mistake again. I've been here with you because I want to be, but I'm not going to beg. So, I'll give you some time to decide whether you want me." He kisses me on the forehead and turns to leave. "Call me when you figure it out."

"I'm pregnant." I yell.

He stops at the door.

"Is it mine or Ava's?" he questions.

"Don't do that. You're making this out to be my fault when you're the one who lied."

"And I owned up to my mistake. What else do you want?"

"I want assurance you're here for me."

"Haven't I been good to you?" he inquires.

"Yes."

"Don't I make you feel good?"

"Yes."

"And you love me?"

"Yes."

"Then stop letting people come between us. I'm where I want to be. Are you?"

"Yes, and I'm sorry." I rush to him, and he steps back. "Please forgive me. I won't doubt you again."

"I know. Now, give daddy a kiss so you can cook me some of that good Sunday dinner."

chapter three
Ava

I thank Christ Jesus our Lord, who has given me strength to do his work. He considered me trustworthy and appointed me to serve him, even though I used to blaspheme the name of Christ. In my insolence, I persecuted his people. But God had mercy on me because I did it in ignorance and unbelief. Oh, how generous and gracious our Lord was! He filled me with the faith and love that come from Christ Jesus.

This is a trustworthy saying, and everyone should accept it: "Christ Jesus came into the world to save sinners"—and I am the worst of them all. But God had mercy on me so that Christ Jesus could use me as a prime example of his great patience with even the worst sinners. Then others will realize that they, too, can believe in him and receive eternal life. All honor and glory to God forever and ever! He is the eternal King, the unseen one who never dies; he alone is God.

"He alone is God. Amen." I read from First Timothy chapter one before closing my eyes to pray.

"God of heaven and earth whose name is holy and worthy to be praised. God, the beginning, the end and creator of all people and things. Father, I appeal to your throne this morning with a grateful heart, thankful to see a new day I get to call my birthday. Not simply in the sense of being born, but today God, I want to start anew. I may not have done all Paul did, but my sins are still sins.

Forgive me, renewing my mind and life as you did for him. Forgive me for any sins, actions, or reactions then help me to forgive. I've put my life into your hands, and I humbly submit all of me to you. You have my permission to cut away what or who doesn't belong, close any doors which will cause me to fight your plan for my life, and cancel any assignments and relationships which will distract me.

Father, I've spent too long being who you didn't create, and now I'm ready to walk the path you designed. Even if you have to change the direction of my life, do it. God, help me to see more of you and less of me. Help me to restart. I'm tired of being broken, fighting battles not mine and being outside of your will. Help me to see who and what is for me, so I don't miss another blessing. Although it has taken me thirty-eight years to get here, forgive my tardiness. I'm ready now. Ready to see what you have for me. By faith I submit this prayer. Amen."

I begin to hum. "I'm free. Praise the Lord, I'm free. No longer bound, no more chains holding me. My soul is resting and it's just another blessing. Praise the Lord, hallelujah, I'm free."

Later on, I'm sitting on the enclosed patio with the fire pit and my cigar lit and music playing waiting on my pizza to be delivered. When I receive the doorbell notification, I open the app.

"What the—

I go inside and open the door.

"Happy birthday." June exclaims walking in with a cake followed by Grant holding up a bottle. "I hope you're ready to party."

"Party? I thought y'all—

"We lied." She smirks. "You didn't think we'd let you celebrate alone, did you?"

"We? June Havana Carson, what did you do?"

"Bae, I think you're in trouble. She called yo whole guvment name." He jokes.

"Hush. She'll be alright. Ava, answer the door."

Reluctantly, I go over and pull it open.

"We heard it's a party going down here tonight. Don't worry, I know the landlord and he's cool with it." Naomi says coming in with a large tray of food followed by Josiah who has his hands up.

"I was not in on this." He laughs and I squint my eyes at him.

Before I can close the door, Larissa and Michael walk up.

"Let us in this thang. We came for the celebration."

"Hold up." Levar calls out rushing up with two pizza boxes. "A little birdie told me you usually celebrate with a meat lovers pizza from Marco's, so I took the honor of picking up your order and adding to it."

"Oh, for pizza, you can definitely come in." He stops and kisses me on the cheek. "Happy birthday Ava."

An hour into the party, June calls everyone into the living room.

"Thank you for allowing us to crash your birthday."

"Um, allowed, really?"

"Allowed, ambushed, they both start with a. We don't have to get caught up in the details." She states causing everyone to laugh. "Ava, whether we've been friends for years or months, you make it easy to love you. With everything you've experienced the last few months and in your lifetime, we wanted to give you space to celebrate the mere fact you made it. Here." She hands me a box. "Happy birthday sister."

I sit on the couch, placing my wine glass on the table and removing the top.

"June." I whisper with tears filling my eyes at the gold-colored frame containing a hand painted divorce decree.

"Today, on your thirty-eighth birthday, we declare you officially divorced from fear, pain, scars, mistakes, abuse, past, self-doubt, low self-esteem, brokenness and what almost destroyed you. Today, you have the chance to begin again."

"You're determined to make me cry." I tell her.

"Before you do, open ours." Naomi says.

"You guys." I blink back tears at the certificate for a photoshoot.

"There's more." Larissa says handing me another envelope containing certificates for hair and makeup.

"Y'all really did all this for me?" I choke back tears. "Meeting you all has been like a dream I hope to never wake up from. There's been plenty of birthdays I've spent alone by force and choice, and I didn't think I'd ever have this. I can't lie. I was skeptical at first thinking there's no way this many folks can be of God and available to me, at the same time. Yet, God proved me wrong."

"That mane bad, ain't he?" Larissa blurts causing everyone to laugh.

"As long as we minus out Trifling Trina." June adds.

"Girl."

"What?" she shrugs. "You know I'm right."

"Seriously. I'm grateful to each of you for all the gifts."

"Wait, there's one more." Levar says pulling out a Tiffany box and there's an audible gasp throughout the room.

chapter four

"Calm down." He laughs. "It isn't an engagement ring. Yet."

He says the last part softly, but within earshot of my hearing.

"Open it." He instructs.

"Oh Levar, this is beautiful." I refer to the butterfly pendant. "Y'all are determined to make me ugly cry." I fan my face.

"Butterflies represent change, hope, life, spiritual rebirth, and transformation. The caterpillar's transformation to a butterfly comes with struggle, yet it's the struggle which allows them to eventually fly. Ava, I pray each time you wear or see this pendant, it'll remind you of how your struggle has now given you the strength to fly."

"Wow." June says now fanning her face. "That was beautiful."

"Dude, now you got these women looking upside our head." Josiah says.

"Thanks a lot." Michael adds slapping him on the arm. "I'm getting another drink."

When they walk into the kitchen, I stand and give Levar a hug.

"I hope it's not too much."

"No, I love it. Thank you."

Turning to join the others, the doorbell sounds.

"This better not be a stripper." I yell out. Opening the door, I'm shocked to see Katrina standing there.

"Um, are you lost?" June asks over my shoulder.

"Ava, I didn't come to start anything. Can we talk?"

"She's busy with her real friends."

"It's okay." I tell June. "Katrina, come in and say what you need too."

She steps inside, looking over my shoulder. I glance back at June who moves a few steps away and folds her arms.

"First, I apologize for interrupting your party. Here." She passes me a bag. "I purchased it before everything happened last week and well, you can decide if you want to keep it or not."

"Thanks."

She stands there.

"Is there something else?"

"Ava, I'm heartbroken over how things are between us. I truly considered you a friend and maybe one day, you'll see I meant no harm towards you."

"Not today though." June says. "Ava, it's time to cut the cake."

Katrina rolls her eyes.

"Thank you for the gift and I, too, considered you a friend. I thank you for everything you did for me, and I wish you much success in your relationship."

Her smile widens. "I knew we could get pass this and I hope it means you'll help us. See, I talked to Don—I mean Andre and he explained why he lied about his name, and I've forgiven him. We're supposed to meet with his lawyer on Monday and I'm—

"Katrina, stop. You misunderstood my statement. I considered, emphasis on the e d. Meaning, past tense. Therefore, I don't want to hear any details of your life with dude. He's in my past and since he's part of your present, we can't be friends. Oh, and the only thing I'll help Andre with is going to jail."

"Wow, so everything I've done for you meant nothing and you rudely dismiss me like I wasn't the one praying you out the funk you were in. Where were your little friends when the enemy was whipping your butt all up and down the street?"

"Here I thought you were doing those things to help and the entire time you were keeping score. How Christian of you."

"And you weren't the only one praying, chicken head. Ava, let Ka-fused out before she's the one getting whipped." June states.

"Hush, nobody is talking to you." She says to June.

"Heifer."

Grant grabs June.

"It's time for you to go."

"And you." Katrina points at me. "You want to play the good Christian after being baptized for twelve hours, yet you're keeping up this lie. Andre never hurt you and the right thing would be dropping the charges against him. Ava, I'm about to have his first child and he deserves to be here with us."

"Hold on." I start searching through the plants and mail I have sitting by the door.

"What are you doing?"

"Looking for the mind you've obviously lost. How dare you bring your narrow ass to my house, on my birthday to advocate for a Negro you barely know. A., the audacity, and b, the ignorance to believe him when he says I lied like there isn't evidence. He tried to kill me." I slowly pronounce. "Not once did he show an ounce of compassion towards me and now you expect me to take his feelings into consideration and drop the charges. Girl, Andre deserves every day he'll spend in prison."

"He said you'd badmouth him."

"Everything concerning Andre is bad, including his mouth. Katrina, you may think Andre hung the moon, but he couldn't hang a picture if his life depended on it. When he drains your bank account, ruins your credit and have you filing bankruptcy for the debt he incurs, like I did, don't show up here. When he destroys your life like he almost destroyed mine, don't call me."

"I get you're upset, but things don't have to be bad between us."

I laugh. "I'm the one crazy to be standing here arguing with a fool. Let me put this as plain as I can. I wouldn't drop the charges if it meant saving humanity. Andre made a choice to do what he did even after I begged him to leave me alone. Therefore, he deserves to be in jail and if you show up here again, you might join him."

I open the door. She steps out and I close it.

"And f you, dude and that bald head baby." June hollers after snatching the door back open.

We all burst into laughter.

"Why the baby got to be bald headed?" Naomi asks through tears.

"Cause he old and I bet the baby is going to look like a little old version of him." She shrugs. "And you need to stop being nice. Chick should have been kicked out the minute you took this lil stanky gift bag. Talking about dropping the charges cause she's having his baby. And trick? Dogs have babies and they still go to the pound. Musty tail got me heated."

"You're right, I shouldn't have entertained her and after tonight, I won't anymore." I tell her while dropping the gift in the garbage. "Now, calm down."

"And I won't hold it against you for choosing to go to church with her, after all the times I've asked." June rolls her eyes.

I go over to her. "I'm sorry, but boo, Repairers of the Breach doesn't last all day like your church. You need lunch and a snack. Stomach be touching your back by the time you leave."

Grant laughs and she cuts her eyes at him.

"Unuh, don't do us. Besides, that was the old church, wanch." She swats at me, and everybody laughs.

"I'll visit yours next." I tell her.

"Whatever. Hand me a slice of pizza."

chapter five
Dr. Greene

"Ava, what are you thankful for? Don't give me the usual, dig deep."

"I used to hate this question." She tells me.

"Why?"

"Truthfully, I never thought I had anything to be thankful for. I grew up in foster care and group homes sharing toys and wearing hand me down clothes and shoes. In college, I was always working through the holidays. Then being with Andre, Thanksgiving was another day for me to cook and him to eat, leaving me to clean up while he watched football."

"What about now?"

"Now, I'm simply grateful to be alive. These last seven months have made me appreciate seeing another birthday, the chance to start again and friends who have quickly become family. Dr. Greene, it's always been me against the world. Yet, God has granted me the blessing of meeting a group of people who don't want anything from me, but me. I've never had that. Well, besides Katrina seeing she's shacking up with my ex."

I let out a gasp.

"Right. Same reaction I had along with some choice words."

"How are you dealing with this?"

"I'm not." She states. "I refuse to give them anymore of my energy. I tried to warn her, but she's love-sick and in the early stages when Andre can get you to do anything he wants. As far as I'm concerned, they can have each other and ride off into the sunset."

"I hear you and it sounds good, but it's not realistic."

"What do you mean?" she questions.

"Ava, refusing not to deal with things won't make them go away. It's like stashing boxes of junk in the attic. Although it's out of sight and out of mind, one of these days you're going to have to deal with it. You shared a number of years with Andre, and you considered Katrina a friend. Regardless of how their relationship came to be, even if yours was over, there has to be a feeling of betrayal and hurt."

"Hurt, yes. Betrayal no. Dr. Greene, I know Andre. He's a smooth talker who can get you to eat ice cream when you know your lactose intolerant. At first, I felt sorry for Katrina because I thought she'd fallen under the spell of his sales pitch. It wasn't until she opened her mouth to defend him, I realize she's the clown. Oh, did I mention she's pregnant? Yeah."

"Does that make you angry?"

"What, him moving on? Heck no. I pray she makes him forget me. They can have each other. Dumb and dumber."

"I meant her being pregnant." I clarify.

"No, it makes me remember the pain of losing a baby, alone because Andre was too busy to show up at the hospital. For ten hours, thirteen minutes and eight seconds, I had to labor and push out my twenty-two-week-old son whose heart stopped beating. For months afterwards, I wished mine had too and the entire time, he never mumbled a word. It would be on the year anniversary of his death, while I scattered his ashes, my anger changed to relief."

"Why relief?"

"My son never had to experience Andre as a father. So, no I'm not angry. I feel sorry for the child who gets them as parents."

"Okay, let's go back to the things you're thankful for. How has it been letting others into your life which means giving them access to your trust card?" I ask her.

"It's hard when it hasn't been used in a while. However, I realize the only way to meet new people, I have to actually meet them." She chuckles.

"Yeah, that's how it works. Ava, you do know not everybody will hurt you, right?"

"I do, but when you've been hurt so much, your mind goes from questioning if they'll hurt you to when will they hurt you. How do I deal with the anxiety while waiting?"

"What if you didn't question at all and simply allow things to play out, enjoying the moments instead of anticipating what'll happen next?"

"I don't know what that looks like."

"Let's say you make plans for tomorrow which include a hike, picnic lunch and swimming. You check the weather forecast and it says there's a small chance of rain. You get up the next day and the sun is shining, although the chance of rain remains. Do you go on about your day or cancel your plans?"

"I'll go on with my plans since there's only a small chance—oh, I see. You're good."

"Ava, there's always a small chance of rain, i.e. something bad happening, in every relationship. It doesn't mean you abandon it. Instead, you make provisions in case the rain happens to show up. Besides, if you canceled your plans every time there's a possibility of rain, you'd never enjoy the outside."

"You're right, Dr. Greene and I'm learning this daily. Truthfully, I love having people in my corner. Friday, my friends showed up, unexpectedly, to celebrate my birthday with food and gifts. It was the first time I've ever had a party as an adult. They don't know this, but I cried like a baby when they left." She laughs.

"As long as they were happy tears. Ava, trusting again is a process. It's letting people in when you're hurting. It's asking someone to help you then letting them do the actual helping. It's not expecting them to do anything wrong yet forgiving them if they do. It's letting them love you and believing they'll do what they say."

"It's hard."

"You know what else is hard?" I inquire.

She shakes her head.

"Being alone when you don't have to be. Don't misunderstand this as being forced to do anything you're uncomfortable with. What I'm suggesting is taking the steps to destroy the walls, created in trauma, in order to not miss who God has placed in your life for a reason or season."

chapter six
Ava

I walk into the church for pre-Thanksgiving service. After the session with Dr. Greene yesterday, I'm more excited about getting on with my life.

"Are you Ms. Ava?"

"Yes, I am, um Jasmine." I strain to see her badge as a youth usher.

"Pastor would like to see you in his office."

"Thanks."

I follow her down the hall, tapping on the door.

"Come in."

I walk in to see him, Lady Hunter, and Deacon Carlisle.

"Good evening, you wanted to see me?"

"Yes, have a seat. How are you?"

"I'm good. If this is about the argument with Katrina, I apologize to you and Lady Hunter. I'm ashamed of how I allowed the conversation to go inside the church. It will not happen again."

"Thank you and although we hope you two have amicably resolve things, it's not what I asked to see you about."

"We talked and decided to leave things as they are. I love her as Christ commands, but we won't be friends. Nevertheless, is there something wrong?"

"In a way, yes." Lady Hunter replies.

"Okay." I look at each of them. "What is it?"

"Last Friday, the church received a letter alluding to you being involved in some, um, how can I put this." She pauses.

"Please speak freely. We're all grown." I tell her.

"The letter insinuates your involvement in showcasing your body on a platform called only fans. These were also included." Deacon passes me some pictures. "As you can see, this is a problem for the church."

"This isn't me and even if it was, why is it a church problem?"

"Sister Ava, you're free to do whatever you like as a grown woman. However, when you make a substantial donation to the church, it becomes a problem. We can't have someone thinking the church is being financed by dirty money." Deacon states.

"Dirty money? Are y'all serious? Sir, I'm not trying to finance the church and neither did I give a donation. I tithed which I thought was the right thing."

"It is." He states.

"Then I'm confused, and it could be due to being new to this Christian journey. But doesn't the Bible instruct us to tithe from our earnings since tithe keeps the church functioning?"

"You're correct." Pastor Hunter finally speaks up. "Tithing isn't a mandatory thing, it's an action of faith and trust."

"Again, a contribution to the church for the upkeep, to pay bills and your salary. Am I wrong?"

"No."

"Okay, then where in your Bible does it say the earnings had to be from a specific field of work? I seemed to have missed it in mine."

"Ava, we're in no way trying to insinuate you're wrong in this matter."

"You did though. This meeting wasn't to make me aware of someone trying to smear my name. Instead, I've been chastised for what you think I do for a living. What if it was me? What if it's what I had to do to make ends meet after losing my job? What if it's the only way I can afford health insurance to pay for cancer or high blood pressure medicine? Neither of you asked if it was me, you just assumed it was because my tithe was more than you're used to."

"We apologize." Pastor says.

"It's cool, but I take it the church is returning my check."

Neither of them says anything.

"Surely, if the church can criticize my career choice, then the church won't accept the money I make doing it, right?"

"Ava, we didn't mean to upset you."

"Well, I am upset." I stand. "I get you wanting your members to represent Jesus but criticizing whatever form of work a person chooses to make a living is sad and hurtful. Especially if it's not a direct reflection on the church or hurting anyone. I've gone through a lot of darkness in my life and becoming a member here felt like I was finally seeing light. Until now. Had either of you looked deeply, you'd see Katrina's mark all over this instead of making me regret doing what I thought was a good thing. And for the record, that check was one of a few I'd planned on giving the church from a lawsuit I won. Now, I'm rethinking it and my membership."

"Ava, wait." Pastor Hunter calls out.

"No sir. I think it's best I leave. Have a great service and Happy Thanksgiving."

I push open the door.

"Oh." Katrina steps back. "Good evening, Ava. You look upset. Was it something I said?" she laughs.

"You don't have the power to upset me. What you do have is too much of the wrong color foundation. You look dead."

I push pass her. Inside the truck, I lock the doors and sit there.

"Father, I will not allow the enemy to trick me out of my position and purpose with you. Maybe I rushed into joining a church home and if that's the case, please lead me to the place which can feed, protect, and guide me spiritually. And God, I forgive them and pray you will too. I can't carry the weight of someone else's burden of foolishness, and neither will I feel bad for trusting in my tithe. I trust you God and I still believe. Amen."

Starting the truck, I put it in reverse and immediately beeping starts. I slam on brakes when I see Katrina standing there. Putting the truck in park, I get out.

"Girl, why are you standing behind my truck?"

"Ah." She sits on the ground and begins to scream. "You tried to run me over."

"Um, there's nobody else out here dummy."

"There will be. Help, somebody help me."

I lean against the truck, clasping my hands in front of me.

A security guard rushes over. "Katrina, what happened? Are you okay?"

"She tried to run me over when all I wanted to do was talk to her." She cries. "Call the police."

Ten minutes later, the police, fire and ambulance have the parking lot covered, along with church security and a few nosey members.

"Ava."

I exhale. "Clay."

"Old girl said you tried to run her over."

"If I wanted to run her over, I would have. However, as you can see, she's perfectly fine, physically. Mentally, well that's a different story."

"She's lying and I want to press charges." Katrina yells with fake tears. "I'm pregnant and she put both of our lives in danger."

"I hate to do this, but you're going to have to come with me until we can get this straightened out."

"Are you kidding me?"

"Unfortunately not." He says, leading me to his patrol car.

chapter seven

While he's gone, I call Jamia to let her know what's happening. A few minutes later, he returns opening the door.

"You're free to go."

"He says I'm free to go." I relay to Jamia. "Yeah, but I don't trust them. Any of them." I look Clay up and down. "They'll wait until I drive away to try and charge me with leaving the scene or something."

"Ava, no one is going to do anything. Katrina isn't pressing charges. The EMTs checked her out and says she's good. You can leave or stay. Your choice. Either way, have a good night."

He walks off and I tell Jamia I'm going to stay. Hanging up with her, I get my purse from the truck, lock it, and walk pass Katrina throwing the middle finger. Inside, I stop by the bathroom. I press my hands on the counter, closing my eyes to calm the anger that's threatening to spill out.

"Hey, are you okay?"

I jump when someone touches me.

"My apologies for startling you." An usher says. "Are you okay?"

"Yes ma'am. Thank you."

"If you need anything, let me know. I'm Rose."

I nod.

Inhaling then exhaling, I wash my hands. "No weapons formed against me will prosper."

In the sanctuary, I sit near the back as one of the associate ministers preaches.

"I had to for real pray about this thang because I couldn't understand why God would let my enemies prosper. Until God checked me, by asking some questions. Like, how do you know I'm the one blessing them, how do you know if they're really prospering, surviving, and happy? Truth is, I didn't know. I assumed since people have become great at pretending.

So, instead of me feeling sorry for what I think of them, God told me to thank them instead. Yeah, He told me to thank folk who took advantage of me since it made me stronger and wiser. I know this might be hard for some of you but in order to move from where you are, you may have to start making amends with folk. Those who hurt you, maliciously used you, abused you, mishandled you and your gifts, lied, and even profited from your suffering.

Yes, on this Thanksgiving eve, you may have to thank those who did you wrong and will never apologize. You may have to thank the one who left you with scars and tried to ruin you. Why? It moves you out the way, leaving room for God's wrath. See, if you continue being angry and trying to get revenge, you're taking matters into your own hands when scripture says, "*Do not take revenge, my dear friends, but leave room for God's wrath.*"

Jesus, in preparation for His crucifixion knew He would be betrayed yet He says at the last supper in Luke 22:21-22, *"But here at this table, sitting among us as a friend, is the man who will betray me. For it has been determined that the Son of Man must die. But what sorrow awaits the one who betrays him."* Jesus didn't need to handle the ones who would betray Him, their sorrow was already written.

Somebody in this place needs to tell the enemy, Negroes on your job, folk in your family, the ex who won't leave you alone, the self-doubt and everything else thank you. Thank you for giving up on me, it made me work harder. Thank you for speaking ill against my life, it allowed me to recognize how valuable I was. Thank you for the times you didn't show up, answer the phone, or support me because you can't take the credit. Thank you, your job is done and I'm no longer allowing you to ruin my victory. Not after the many nights spent in pain, days of crying and struggling, months of trying to press beyond the depression, suicidal thoughts, addictions, anger, abuse, hurt and losses. Baby, take this thank you and get gone cause this new person, you won't like. She fights back."

I stand with my hands lifted as tears stream.

"Somebody, tell your neighbor, I ain't the same. The old me took it, but the new me is saying, I'm knuckin', buckin' and ready to fight."

chapter eight
Andre

I pull up to the church on two wheels. "Get in." I yell out the window at Katrina.

She stops to talk to the security dude, and I lay on the horn.

"What is wrong with you?" she questions once inside the car.

"Are you seriously asking me this after laying your stupid ass behind that lady's truck? Why Trina, huh? Why?"

"I thought if she got arrested, we could use it to make her drop the charges."

"We? We ain't the one in this mess and if she tells them folks I'm harassing her, they can revoke my bail. Is that what you want?"

"Of course not. I'm sorry."

She tries to touch me, and I pull away. "I don't know how much more of this I can take. Ever since you found out who I am, all your talk is Ava. I'm beginning to think you want her more than me."

"That's not fair."

"What's not fair is me going to jail because of you."

"Really?" she laughs. "Negro, I'm not the one who has your balls in a vice grip. You should be mad at her, not me."

"I'm handling Ava, but you're making things worse. For the final time, leave Ava alone."

"Wow. You're in love with her."

"Please don't start."

"Admit it. You love her."

"Yes." I say hitting the steering wheel. "Of course I love her. She was a part of my life for over thirteen years, but she's my past and you're supposed to be my future."

"What are you saying?" she asks with tears.

"I don't know if this is something we should continue."

"You're breaking up with me over this?"

"Shouldn't I? You don't seem to get how bad things can get for me. I'm trying to get Ava to drop the charges and you're out here acting like we're in Junior High."

"I'm sorry. I saw her and she said my foundation makes me look dead. It made me mad, and I overreacted without thinking."

"That's evident. Hell, it ain't her fault you didn't match the shit with your skin. Now, my boys on the force laughing like I'm some joke. Get out of my car."

"Where are you going? Babe, please talk to me."

"I'm going to stay at my place tonight to give you time to reflect on what you've done."

"I'm not a child who needs time out." She sternly states.

"Then stop acting like one."

"Andre—

"Get out Trina."

She slams my door before stomping off. I follow her out of the church parking lot, doubling back once I ensure she's gone. Parking away from Ava's truck, I wait. A little time passes, and I finally see the lights flash. When she leaves, I follow her.

She stops at Kroger. I park, jumping out.

"Ava."

Quickly turning, I notice her hand goes to her waist.

"You're carrying?"

"You want to find out?" she challenges.

"I'm not a threat to you. I only came to apologize for the stunt Katrina pulled. You may not believe me, but I had no parts in it. She's trying anything to get you to drop the charges in order to have me here for the baby."

"The baby." She chuckles. "You expect me to act like nothing happened so you and Katrina can be a happy family? I think not. I wouldn't care if she was carrying

John the Baptist reincarnated. Whatever you and Thumbelina got going, leave me out of it."

"Ava, I love you."

"You don't love me and I'm no longer the fool believing you can. You only have the capacity to love yourself and Marble wobbly tail."

"You don't have to talk about my mother."

"Dude, I'm trying to forget you and your mammy, praying you'll return the favor and forget me too."

"Look Ava." I step closer to her.

"No, Andre." She sighs putting her hands up and taking a step back. "Please let me be."

"How can I do that with this criminal case over my head."

"You act like I did this." She bellows. "You made the choice to wrap your hands around my throat and now, I'm supposed to make your life easier by dropping the charges. Screw you and your mentally ill girlfriend."

"I'm sorry and I'll regret what I did for the rest of my life, but I shouldn't have to spend the next fifteen years in jail. It's embarrassing enough I've lost my job and had to watch IAB go through my house, removing my uniforms. What more do you want?"

"I want you to pay for what you did." She screams. "You don't get to inflict the pain then decide what the punishment should be. If you ask me, fifteen years isn't long enough. Not when you've sentenced me to a lifetime of remembering what you did. Dre, please leave me alone."

"You're really going to be a bitch? We both know things didn't have to get this far."

She turns back laughing. "Wow. Do you hear yourself? What the fu—what is wrong with you? Things didn't have to get this far. You're right, nigga. They didn't. Yet, you act like I invited this when you were the one who broke into my home, attacked, and raped me. You! This is all on you. At what point are you going to take responsibility?"

"I'm trying too, but I can't go to jail for fifteen years. Will you at least ask the prosecutor to drop the rape?" I ask. "Please."

"You're really standing here with a straight face asking me to again sacrifice my life for yours. You know what, sure that's what I'll do."

"Really?"

"Yep, as soon as you drop off the face of the earth. Call me when it happens."

"Ava." I yell and she throws the middle finger over her shoulder.

chapter nine
Ava

"Happy Thanksgiving." June exclaims when I walk into her kitchen.

"Happy Thanksgiving sis. Where do you want this?" referring to the pan of macaroni and cheese.

"Hold up. What's with the mood?"

"First, I need a glass of wine." I go over, sit the pan on the stove then get a glass. "You want one."

"No thanks." She smiles.

"You're not drinking? What's up?"

"I haven't been drinking the last five months." She pulls her shirt back and I squeal.

"Oh my God. June." I tear up. "You're pregnant?"

She nods up and down with her own set of tears.

"Five months today. Ava, this is Tru Abigail Carson who'll be here to meet you in April 2022." She rubs her stomach.

"A girl. June." I pull her into a hug. "Why didn't you tell me?"

"We wanted to make it pass the first trimester and with everything going on, I didn't want you worrying about me."

"Is everything good? What is the doctor saying? Are there any complications? Is she healthy? Are you? Tell me."

"Calm down Grant Jr." She swats my hand away. "Everything is great and there's been no issues this time. We're already declaring her healthy and full term."

June has been pregnant three times resulting in three miscarriages. The last one she made it to fourteen weeks and when she lost her, I thought I was going to lose her too. Each time she had bleeding early on and had to be on bed rest. This is the first time she's had no complications.

"Praise God. Auntie can't wait to meet you sweet girl." I kiss her stomach. "Are we keeping it a secret?"

"No. We plan to announce it to our families tonight. This has been a long time coming, but for her it's worth it."

"Amen. Oh, I'm so happy. I can't wait to start shopping."

"Oh Lord. Ava do not go overboard. Who am I kidding? Well, can you at least wait until you've found a house?"

"Maybe. Ooh, I know the perfect person to create her nursery. What's the theme? Never mind, I'll ask Grant. He's better with this kind of thing."

She rolls her eyes. "Whatever. Tell me what has you in a funk."

"Had. I'm better now, but yesterday was a doozy." I reply pouring wine. "You're probably going to wish for a glass after you hear this."

I tell her about the meeting at church, the bogus runover with Katrina and the conversation with Andre.

"Andre and Katrina are pitiful. They need a good old fashioned big momma whooping with a switch."

"They also need to leave me alone."

"Hopefully, it won't be much longer before all of this is over, and Andre's tail is in jail. Maybe then you'll get the peace you desperately need and the chance to start over fresh."

"From your lips to God's ears." I tell her.

"Speaking of God. I'm so disappointed in Repairers of the Breach. This kind of foolery is another reason people no longer trust the assembly of church. Hell, even if you were showcasing your assets for the world, it's your prerogative and doesn't stop your money from paying the church's electric bill."

"Right. But the problem I have, they were more concerned with my supposed career choice than someone, aka Katrina, smearing my name. What hurts the most, I really thought I'd found a church home."

"Well, don't allow one bad experience to change your expectation of church. They're some great ones left, including the one I attend. Hint, hint. So, take some time and date a few churches until you find the right one for you."

"Date?"

"Yeah. Your church home is like a relationship. It should love, feed, comfort, protect and know how to handle you when you're hurt. Sis, when you've been wounded by the world, the place you call your church home should be capable of bandaging you. Therefore, you should be as picky and thorough about it as you would your man."

"I never thought of it like that."

"Hence the reason you have me."

"I wouldn't know what to do without you."

"God willing, you'll never have to. Okay, okay. Enough of this mushy stuff. What are you going to do about Lil Puff, Coco and the bald head baby?"

I spit out my wine laughing.

"June."

"Child, we both know they're a few puffs short of a pull." She shrugs.

"You ain't never lied." I chuckle. "But as bad as I want to use my hands and words, I'm going to let the law handle them. I've lost enough fooling with them. I won't allow them to take my freedom nor sanity too. I have to believe God will handle it."

"He will. However, be careful. If this chick will go as far as to lay down behind your truck, there's no telling what she'll do."

"I am."

After dinner with June, Grant, and their families, I'm home showered and in my pajamas. Sitting in the middle of the bed with my laptop, notebook, and pen, I decide to look for a new house as a Christmas gift to myself. I spend an hour making a list of a few to check out before looking at some baby websites. It's almost midnight when I close the laptop and grab the remote to watch an episode of SWAT. I jump when I hear a thud next door. Pausing the TV, I wait. Shrugging it off to something falling, I press play and slide under the covers.

Beeping

I'm jolted from my sleep by the smoke detector and the blaring sounds of the alarm. Sitting up, I immediately begin to cough.

"Oh my God."

Pulling the shirt up over my nose, I can barely make out my hand in front of me. Feeling for my phone, I find it and dial 911. Putting it on speaker, I crawl to the door.

"Oh my God." I rush back into the room, slamming the door.

"911, what's the address of your emergency?"

"1278 Virginia Avenue, and my house is on fire." I yell to the operator.

"Okay. Can you tell me your name and is anyone else in the house with you?"

"Ava Gentry and no ma'am."

"Do you know where the fire is coming from?"

Coughing. "I believe it's in the living room."

"Where are you in the home and can you get out?" she asks.

"In the bedroom on the far-right side of the house, near the back. I'm going to try the window." Coughing. "I'm almost there." Reaching it, I lay the phone on the windowsill and feel around for the latch. "The window is up." I grunt, pushing with all my might to get the screen off. Finally, I push the phone out then hoist myself up and out the window. Hitting the ground hard enough to take my breath.

"I'm out." I tell her. "Thank you, God."

Sometime later, I open my eyes to see I'm in the back of the ambulance.

"Ava. Hey, it's Josiah. Can you hear me?"

I nod, removing the oxygen from my face and bursting into tears.

"I can't catch a break. I'm so sorry Josiah."

"Ava, this isn't your fault. Material things can be replaced which is why we pay insurance."

"I know, but it seems like every time good happens, evil strips it away. I'm tired of losing."

He takes my hand, and I cry harder.

"When a runner is nearing the end of their race, they're fatigued, lungs hurting, and muscles tighten. Yet, some of them experience what's called a second wind. Some scientists believe an increase in endorphins kills the pain signals to help deal with difficult physical activities. Ava, I don't know when your second wind will kick in, but the only way it can you have to keep running. While you do, continue to increase your faith, especially during the most painful trials knowing they have to end eventually. Stay the course. Let's pray."

"Excuse me. Are you Ms. Gentry?" a woman asks.

I sit up on the gurney. "I am and this is Josiah Rainey, my landlord and owner of the property."

"Sir and ma'am, my name is Chief Maurice Payne, and this is Fire Inspector, Lieutenant Brielle Perkins. First, are you okay?"

"Yes, thank you. I was given oxygen as a precaution. Was there a lot of damage?" I inquire.

"Unfortunately, yes. The property sustained a lot of damage along the wall that is shared between the two spaces, the living area and some of the bedroom. We were able to extinguish it before it engulfed the entire dwelling, but what wasn't burned incurred major smoke damage."

"Is there anything salvageable?" I ask.

"I don't believe so, but we can't be sure until we've had a chance to walk through."

"Oh God."

"I'm so sorry." She tells me.

"Do you know what started it?" Josiah asks.

"Preliminary findings suggest your neighbor was using a heater, and one ignited the curtains in the living room."

"That's not possible." I tell them. "He's out of town for the holiday."

"Maybe he returned early." Josiah says. "I'll call him."

"You may want to hold off. If it was him, I'm sorry to say, but he perished in the fire." Lt. Perkins informs us.

chapter ten

"Are you sure it's him?"

"No sir, not until there's a formal identification by the medical examiner."

"Jesus. Do you all mind if I say a quick prayer?" Josiah queries and everyone shakes their heads.

"Father, while we thank you for the sparing of one life, I pray you accepted the soul of another into your bosom on tonight. God, I ask you comfort the family of the departed as they begin the grief process and may they find strength and peace in you. Then God, restore everything lost. Thank you for these firefighters tonight. Bless and keep them safe. Amen."

"Amen."

"Here's my card." Lt. Perkins says. "Someone from my office will be in touch once the investigation is complete. You'll be able to receive a copy of the report for your insurance company. In the meantime, if you have any questions, don't hesitate to contact me and if you need resources, the Red Cross is available."

"Do you know when I'll be able to see if anything survived the fire?"

"Give us a few days. We'll board the dwelling to ensure no one can get in and will let you know when it's safe." She replies.

"What about my truck?"

"It wasn't damaged. However it'll be hours before you're able to move it. When you can, I'll send someone over to assist."

"Thanks." I exhale as she walks away. "Josiah, do you think this could have been Andre or Katrina's doing?"

"Why would they set fire to your neighbor's house?"

"I don't know. Maybe hoping I'd be collateral damage."

"Do you really think they'd go this far?"

"I wouldn't put it past them. Katrina tried to have me arrested for running her over last night after laying down behind my truck. Then Andre followed me to the grocery store to convince me to drop the charges."

"Did you call the police?"

"Katrina did, but it was Andre's friends who showed up." I tell him.

"Ava don't ever give them the benefit of the doubt. Any time Andre breaks the conditions of his bond and the protection order, have him arrested. If Katrina keeps showing up, have her thrown in jail too."

"You're right and I will."

"I'm going to inform Lt. Perkins and see if they can find anything while they investigate. For now, let's get you out of the cold."

Three hours later, I'm checked in at the Hampton Inn after stopping by Walmart. Thank God, the contents of my purse weren't destroyed, and Lt. Perkins allowed me to get it. I'm also grateful for sleeping in pajamas and the pair of boots in my truck. After showering and washing my hair, I'm staring at the ceiling unable to sleep.

"Lord, thank you for sparing my life. I realize the current circumstances could cause me to lose hope, yet I won't stop praying. Praying for peace, protection, prosperity, purpose, and the right people around me. Father don't allow me to miss your plans for my life by looking through lenses of the past. Strengthen me, by your might so I do not fall into old patterns of shacking with fear. God I am yours and I belong to you, therefore I will not pay evil for evil, count myself out, be led astray by what I see nor lose my joy. Instead, I'm going to let you be God, committing my life to you, trusting your will and plan." Sighing.

"In every circumstance, I shall be thankful. House destroyed by fire, I'm still thankful I got my life. Court case hanging over my head, I'm thankful you'll deal with my enemies. Evilness has overtaken who used to be a friend, I'm thankful you allowed me to see it. In every circumstance, I am thankful knowing you got my back. In the name of Jesus, I pray. Amen."

I roll over to the sound of my vibrating phone. Picking it up, I stop the alarm and drag myself to the side of the bed. After a shower and getting dressed, I grab my purse. Opening the door, I gasp when a knife is punched into my stomach.

"You didn't think this was over, did you?"

I jump up, realizing it was a nightmare.

"Oh God." I wipe my hand over my face. "God, I rebuke the hand of death and evilness from my life. Deal with my enemies, God and keep me safe. Amen."

───────────────

I jerk up when I feel someone sit on the side of the bed.

"Who are you?"

"Don't be afraid Ava, I'm not here to hurt you."

"Who are you?" I ask again. "How did you get in here?"

"A friend coming to check on you. Everybody is worried. It's been three days since you've left this room."

"I'm fine." I lie.

"You're not fine and that's okay. You suffered another major loss which can knock the wind out of the strongest person. Yet, you have to get up."

"Why? What's the point of getting up only to face another day of disaster and pain? I'm tired and it feels like I'm fighting for nothing."

"This isn't what you prayed last night."

"How do you know what I prayed? Oh." I pause. "Well look Angel dude, tell God I meant every word last night, but right now, I don't feel like being holy or getting up."

"How long will you mourn what you've lost?" he asks. "Do you not know God has the power to restore?"

"Yes. Yes, I'm aware of God's power, but it still doesn't make it easy to deal with pain like this. I'm tired."

"Ava, this isn't the first time you've suffered a loss, felt pain, or found it hard to breathe and each time you've gotten up. Like those times, getting up after this is going to be one of the hardest things you'll have to do. If you don't, you might not survive."

"Thanks. I'll take it into consideration."

"Ava, much as it hurts, you have to know surviving takes more than faith. What if the woman with an issue of blood refused to get up the morning she touched Jesus' hem? What if the man who'd been lame for 38 years decided not to be taken to the pool of Bethesda the day he'd encounter Jesus? What if Bartimaeus, blind from birth, had decided not to get up the morning he yelled out for Jesus to heal him? Ava, what if you decided not to get up after all those times you've been hurt in the past?"

I swing my legs over the side of the bed. "No offense, but I don't want to hear this right now. I'm angry and I have the right to be."

"You do, but then what? After the anger subsides, you'll still have to face this."

"I know anger doesn't fix it, but it's all I have right now." I yell standing. "I'm the one who lost everything again."

"You didn't lose your life."

"Gee, what a life." I mock. "Thank you for coming. You may leave now."

He sits there.

I go over and snatch the door open. "Get out!"

"No." He calmly states. "Since you were a child, you're used to people leaving you to fight things alone. Your mother left you to fight grandmother. Grandmother left you to fight granddaddy. Granddaddy left you to fight the system. The system left you to fight Andre. All of those things almost destroyed Ava, but almost means not quite. In other words, they didn't succeed and there's hope of restoration. All you have to do is get up."

I blink and he's standing directly in front of me.

"Get up Ava."

My eyes fly open, and I jump up.

"Whoa. Ava, hey. It's June."

I look around realizing I'm still in bed. My forehead creases with confusion.

"Are you okay?" she asks.

"What happened? How did I get back in bed?"

"What do you mean? You were already in bed. The manager let me in when I explained how worried I was."

I burst into tears.

chapter eleven

I walk out of the bathroom to see June sitting at the table.

"Are you okay?" she asks.

"No." I offer a weak smile. "I'm angry June. At me, Andre, Katrina, God, life dot, dot, dot and I'm scared it's going to consume me."

"It won't if you don't allow it too."

"I'm trying, but when will this end." I yell.

She gets up, goes over to the bed and grabs a pillow. "Here."

"What's this for?"

"To scream into."

"I don't need to."

"Ava, scream."

I glance at her before placing the pillow to my face and screaming. I lower the pillow then put it back, screaming again. This time, falling to my knees to give it all I got.

"Lord, I'm tired." I yell into the pillow. "I'm tired. I'm tired. I'm tired. Tired of being broken, angry, homeless, starting over and singing the same sad lyrics of a song that seems to never end."

June rubs my back and after a few minutes, I sit up leaning against the bed.

"Broken is better than destroyed, anger can be released, you aren't homeless and starting over is okay as long as you have purpose. And sis, you can change the lyrics whenever you're ready." She tells me.

"Part of the problem, I don't know what my purpose is. In my twenties, it was fighting to survive the hand I'd been dealt, finish college, get a decent job and out of a rooming house. Now at almost forty, it feels like I'm fighting some of the same demons. The only difference, I've gone from a rooming house to a hotel while still trying to survive shit I never asked for. Excuse the language."

"Then let's do something about it. Come on."

"Where are we going?"

"For food. You need to eat. You're going to need your strength." She orders.

"For what?"

"Getting up."

"What did you say?"

"I said you need to eat for the strength to get up. Why?"

"This is going to sound crazy, but before you woke me, I had a vision of an angel sitting on my bed telling me to get up. He said getting up will be the hardest thing I do and if I don't, I probably won't survive."

"Wise counsel. You know in first Kings nineteen, Elijah was sitting under a tree begging God to take his life after he'd done what God commanded. He told God he'd had enough of this life and didn't feel he was any better than the ancestors who'd died before him. You know what God did? He had an angel tell him to get up and eat."

"Did he?" I inquire.

"Yes, then he fell asleep again. Yet, God didn't leave him alone. He had the angel to wake him a second time. This time he told him, "*Get up and eat some more, or the journey ahead will be too much for you.*" Like you Elijah didn't know what was before Him. He had no idea he'd have to travel for forty days and forty nights, but God did and had Elijah not eaten, his body would have given out. Sometimes, the preparation God takes us through isn't for what we see, it's for where God has prepared for us. Ava, none of us know what our journey truly consists of. Even with setting goals and making plans with cutout pictures pasted on a poster board, God can come in and shift everything. We survive the shift by having the strength to handle it, the faith to be standing when it's over and the trust to know God is good at what He does."

"Thank you and I apologize for ignoring you. I needed time."

"I tried to give you space, but three days was my max."

I go into the bathroom to rewash my face. Standing in the mirror, I glance at my reflection.

"Can I ask you something?" I question June.

"Sure."

"This past year, everyone I've met has been willing to help me, in some way or another. Each of you have shown me God in different ways and sometimes I think it's too good to be true. Is it realistic to believe it's common for so many people to truly love God?"

"Why is it hard to believe it isn't?"

I step to the door. "Are you really going to answer with a question?"

She laughs. "Seriously Ava, why do we doubt what God can do for His children who are in need? Sometimes, it takes more than one sign to believe, especially when you've had the kind of hurt which causes your trust to be almost nonexistent. Just like it takes a village to raise children, it also takes one to heal. Yes, one can challenge if it's realistic for everyone you meet to be Godly. However, I know it's possible and maybe, He knew you'd need a little from everybody He's placed in your path, even if their presence is momentary."

"You're right. I guess having time to think also gave me time to question things that didn't need to be."

"Questioning isn't bad when you're asking the right ones. Ava, I wholeheartedly believe there are a lot of us who love God and willing to share Him. You happened to meet a handful at the same time, and I consider it a blessing."

I go over pulling her into a hug. "Thank you for not giving up on me."

"You're worth the fight."

Going over to get my purse, I stop clasping my hands in front of me. "Dear God, help me see hope beyond where I am. Give me strength for the journey ahead even if I don't know where it's leading. Don't allow my flesh to overshadow my trust in you. Amen."

"Amen. Now, let's go eat."

chapter twelve

A couple days later I'm walking through the townhouse after the fire department gave us authorization to do so. Naomi and Josiah are next door with an insurance adjuster and fire inspector.

"Man." I sigh standing in the middle of the charred living room before carefully making my way to the kitchen then the bedroom. Glancing over everything, tears fall remembering how great it felt to move in and start over. "Now, I have to do it again."

Walking inside what's left of the closet, I run my hand across the fragments of my clothes and shoes. Near the back, I reach for the burned metal box containing the few personal items I kept of my childhood. Prying it open, everything is destroyed except a half-burned picture of me asleep in my grandfather's arms. I turn it over to see the date on the back.

11/19/1985.

My second birthday and a few months before my mother died.

"Anything worth savaging?" Naomi asks causing me to jump. "Sorry, didn't mean to scare you."

"It's not you. I've been jumpier lately."

"Rightfully so." She says coming over and touching my arm.

"This is the only thing not destroyed."

She takes it.

"A picture of me and the man who'd—no." I abruptly stop. "I'm sorry. My grandfather caused a lot of pain and I have no more space in my head or heart for those dark memories."

She hands it back and I take one last glance before dropping it into the pile and wiping my face.

"I'm sorry Ava."

"Me too." I somberly reply. "But no sense of crying over what was. I have to believe there's a remnant of hope in rebuilding."

"There definitely is."

Making it back to the front, Josiah rushes in.

"Babe, what is it?" Naomi asks.

He points to the door and in walks Alvin Warren.

"Alvin?" she and I both say.

An hour later, we're down at Fire Headquarters.

"I don't understand." Alvin is pacing at the front of the room. "You mean to tell me someone died in my house."

"Yes." We all say for the fifth time.

"I go on a 14-day Australian cruise for the first time in my sixty years of living, only to return home to this. Do y'all know who the unlucky bastard is?"

"That's what we're trying to find out, Mr. Warren." Fire Investigator Kevin Mason replies. "Until dental records can confirm identity, we're at a loss. However, we do know it was a man." He clicks a small remote and images appear on a screen. "If you look here you'll see the remains of an old oil-based heater sitting too close to the curtains."

"Yeah, that's old Sue." Alvin smiles. "She's gotten me through a lot of cold, tough times."

"The heater ignited the curtains, and it'll appear the deceased had a glass of liquor in his hands which must have dropped when the fire started causing him to frantically fling around the room. In doing so, the fire spread quickly throughout the living area."

"And I, well we lost everything." He slumps in the chair. "The only reason I went on this cruise is because it was a retirement gift from the company. Now, I wished I'd stayed my black ass at home."

Naomi touches his arm.

"Mr. Warren, does anyone have a key to your apartment?" Lt. Perkins asks.

"No, only me and Mr. Rainey. I don't have any family and I dang sho ain't got no friends I trust that much."

"Who knew you'd be away?"

"Ava and the mailman."

"Ms. Gentry, did you see or hear anything suspicious before the fire started?"

"No. Wait, yes I did. Around eleven, I heard what sounded like something falling next door, but after pausing the TV and not hearing anything else, I thought maybe something fell. I knew Mr. Warren was out of town and didn't think anything of it. A few hours later, I was awakened by the smoke alarm and my house being on fire."

"Eddie." Mr. Warren blurts, and everyone looks at him. "We used to work together at Kellogg's, and he slept on my couch when he and the wife would get into it. See, he drank a lot, but that's been years ago. I ain't heard from him since I retired last year."

"Did he have a key?"

"Yeah, and I guess he could have kept it, but like I said, it's been a while."

"Can you write his full name down for me?"

———————————

"See, I told you there's nothing to worry about." June reassures as I pace in her living room.

"We won't know for sure until they identify the man who died."

"Ava, stop doing this. You're going to drive yourself crazy with the what ifs."

"I know, but what if they hired this guy, and he got the address mixed up. No. They thought since Mr. Warren wasn't home it'd be easier to start the fire there hoping I wouldn't wake up in time."

She pats the couch next to her. I sit and sigh.

"I know what you're going to say. I need to move on."

"Yeah, you do. You also need to stop watching Lifetime, sis."

I bump her with my shoulder and laugh.

chapter thirteen
Katrina

Fire officials are still investigating the cause of a suspicious fire, on Thanksgiving, which claimed the life of a person who's yet to be identified. Sources within the department say the fire could have been started by a heater but would not give more details.

"What is that?" Andre asks peering over my shoulder.

"The news. Apparently, there was a fire over on Virginia Avenue Thanksgiving night and somebody died. You know where that is?"

"No. Why?"

"Nothing. Where are you headed?"

"To meet my lawyer. Were you able to get my bills straightened out? Ava left me in a bind and everything else is tied up in lawyer fees. I never should have trusted her with my finances."

"Babe, stop worrying." I tell him getting up and wrapping my arms around his waist. "You have me now and I'm making sure you're straight. Plus, with the money you're going to transfer into my account, I can pay all the bills ahead a month while recouping some of what I had to take from my savings."

He moves away. "I know I owe you, Trina. You don't have to keep throwing it in my face. I told you I'll pay you as soon as I get the check from my 401k, but if it's a problem I—

"Hold on, that's not what I'm doing. Why do you get upset every time we talk about finances?"

"It's your tone. You act like I'm some broke bum who can't take care of himself."

"Dre, please don't start with the "everybody is against me," speech. I only mentioned it so you wouldn't forget."

"How can I when it's all you talk about? I have to go."

"Wait, will you be back in time to meet with the appraiser?"

"Appraiser?"

"Yes, appraiser. To see how much this house is worth. We talked about putting it on the market, remember?"

"No, you talked about it. I'm not selling my house." He states.

"Why not? You're at my place all the time anyway. Plus, with the baby coming and the possibility you may have to go away, it makes more sense for us to have one house."

"Then sell yours. My grandmother left me this house."

"I can tell." I scrunch my nose. "Baby, if we sell it while the market is hot, there's a potential to get a lot more than what it's worth. Added bonus, it'll pay off the second mortgage."

"You keep saying we. We aren't selling my house and we don't have time for this with the trial looming over my head."

"The trial is even more reason to get things squared away. Besides, you said the trial isn't a big deal since you aren't guilty, right. Right, Andre?"

"Trina, I don't have time for this. Find something else productive to do, like your hair. The natural look isn't becoming on you."

"You liked it on Ava."

"You ain't her."

He walks out and I rush into the bathroom to look at my hair. An hour later, I'm sitting in my cousin's chair to get a wig put on.

"Katrina, girl where have you been?" Raquel asks.

"Working and taking care of my new man."

"Okay sis. No wonder you're glowing. Who is he?" she swings the chair around. "Spill it."

"His name is Andre. He's a police officer with no baby mommas or crazy exes and he has his own house and car. It's only been a few months, but I can see myself with him for the long term."

"Wait. He isn't the one who attacked the chick some months back, is he?"

"Girl, no. You know I wouldn't mess with somebody like that."

"Good. Anyway, I'm happy for you cousin. You're definitely wearing love well."

"It's not only love." I smirk rubbing my stomach.

"You're pregnant?"

I nod.

"By him?"

"Yes. Why are you saying it like he's an alien or something?"

"Nothing cousin. I'm happy for you."

"But?" I ask looking at her through the mirror.

"Be careful. Police officers can be crazy, controlling, and narcissistic."

"Not my man." I assure her.

"I'm not saying all, but some of them are hiding underline PTSD, depression, debt, criminal histories and everything else. If not, they have this superior, cape wearing complex which makes them think they're saving you."

I shake my head. "Not mine."

"Just be careful and cautious." She tells me.

"Always."

A few hours later, I'm walking out of the salon when I see Ava talking to a guy down the walkway. I get a little closer and hear him congratulating her. When they head inside the pizza café, I follow sliding into a booth behind them.

"Are you excited about the baby?" he asks her and the air catches in my throat.

"Yes, bubbling over excited." She laughs and I roll my eyes. "Lord knows it was a surprise, but I'm taking it as a sign that things are starting to look up."

"Amen. Is it a secret?"

"Not really. It was announced during Thanksgiving dinner, and it may even be on Facebook. Anyway, those who don't will find out at the baby shower. Okay, so I asked you to meet because I need your expertise for the nursery. With everything I'm picturing in my head, you're the only one who can do it. I want the grandest of everything for this little one."

"Ava, girl I got you. When are you thinking of starting?"

"After the holidays. I need to discuss some things with the dad. However, I know how booked you get at the beginning of the year and wanted to put my dibs in first."

"Cool. I'm wrapping up a project and should be done by then. Let's discuss designs."

"Ma'am, hi, hello. I'm Tess. Can I get you something to drink?"

"Water."

"May I suggest an appetizer of mozzarella sticks, fried pickles or onion rings?"

"No thanks."

When she walks off, I grab my stuff and sneak out. Getting to the car, I scream.

"You won't be discussing nothing with my man. Not if I can help it." I start the car, driving around until I see her truck. Parking close to it, I put the car in park and wait.

A car horn blares, and I jolt up, looking around realizing I fell asleep in the car waiting on Ava to come out. Looking at my watch, it's been almost four hours.

"Dang it." I try to start the car and it won't, realizing I'm out of gas.

Hurriedly grabbing my cell phone, I'm taken back by the fact there aren't any missed calls from Andre. I call him and he doesn't answer. Swiping down, I see notifications from Instagram.

(kgaskinsrealtor): ava_gentry83 just shared a post.

I click on it and scoff at the picture with the caption, *'excitedly waiting on the blessings God is preparing for this girl.'*

"Not if I can help it." I state dropping the phone in my lap and hitting the steering wheel.

chapter fourteen
Andre

I ignore the fifth call from Katrina before walking out onto my mother's back porch to see her smoking weed.

"Marble."

"Boy, what have I told you about calling me by my first name? I'm the mother." She gripes.

"Lady please. You ain't never been a mother. A mother would be there when her only son needs her."

"Look Negro don't come in my house with your sour mood. I ain't the reason you're in this predicament. I told you to leave that girl alone when you met her. Instead you wanted to be captain save-a-mutt and now you're wrapped up in all this legal crap."

"I don't need the lecture." I snatch the blunt from her and pull on it. "I only came to pick up the check for the lawyer."

"You didn't have to see me for that. It's on the counter."

I blow out the smoke.

"Are you supposed to be smoking?"

"What else do I have to do?" I hand it back to her. "It's not like I have a job or the ability to get one."

"Only you would get fired on your off-day Craig." She laughs referring to the scene from Friday, the movie.

"Does it look like I'm in the mood for jokes?"

"Then what are you in the mood for? I know it's not to spend time with me, I don't like you like that."

I roll my eyes. "The prosecutor offered me another deal."

"What is it this time?"

"Fifteen years at thirty-three percent with the remaining time on parole."

She doesn't say anything instead blows out smoke.

"Well?"

"Well, what?" she asks. "What do you want me to say?"

"I don't know why I even came here to get advice from you. I've been dealing with this mess for months on my own."

She blows out smoke again.

"Goodbye Marble."

"Oh, did you expect me to stroke your back while you were whining like a girl? Dude, compassion for stupid ain't never been my ministry."

"Being a mother hasn't either."

She laughs.

"Boy, you can't hurt my feelings with anything you got to say about me. You expected me to drop everything and come running to your side when I didn't tell you to beat that girl. Should have learned to keep your hands to yourself or hit low so it doesn't show."

"From whom, you?" I yell. "Nobody ever taught you."

"Lower your tone before I knock you on your ass Andre."

"I don't know why I bother with you."

"You need my money, dummy. How else can you afford to keep that old raggedy house now that your meal barrel done rolled off and found some sense?" she chuckles joking on the weed.

"Are you done?"

"Nigguh, you the one acting like a little girl with all the dramatics. Hell, I was sitting out here enjoying my good weed and Jack until you brought all this negativity."

I sit back in the chair. "I don't know what to do." I admit.

"If you want my honest opinion, I say take the deal. We both know you're guilty and five years is a slap on the wrist."

"I didn't rape her."

She laughs again. "Is lying to yourself helping you sleep? Boy, you've been taking what isn't yours since you were little. I know, I taught you. Only, you've seemed to have forgotten the rules."

"Your famous rules." I scoff.

"You got-doggone right and they ain't failed me yet. Wouldn't have failed you either, had you listened. I've always told you. The most important rule is never stay in a place too long, get what you need and get out. But noooo, you got comfortable thinking that girl belonged to you, giving her a chance to wake up and realize she could do so much better. You should have treated her like property. Used her then replaced her."

"At least she tried to keep a house. It's more than I can say about you." I angrily reply.

"You're almost fifty and continue harping over stuff from when you were a child. Hell, you didn't die, go hungry or lack for anything otherwise you wouldn't be here today. So, stop blaming me for your decisions when there were choices to do better. Yes, I made some mistakes with you, but I did the best I could."

"Lady, I think you need to look up the definition of best. I'm pretty sure it isn't beating the hell out of your child, leaving them alone for days or teaching them how to swindle folks while in elementary."

"You ain't the first person to get beat. My momma hit me if the wind blew too hard, yet I survived and so did you."

"This ain't surviving Marble." I yell. "I'm facing prison."

She stands up, stopping in front of me. When I look up, she slaps me, and I jump from the chair.

"If you feel froggy nigga, leap." She punches me in the stomach. "Since when did I raise a punk?" she hits me again. "Are you wearing panties now? Turn around and let me see."

"Ah." I scream out. "Stop."

"Answer me."

"No."

"Then man up. You a whole grown ass man who made the choice to put your hands on a woman with witnesses around and now you want me to feel sorry for you. I told you to leave that girl at the rooming house she was living in, but you went to rescue the mut and now you can't cry about the fleas."

"What am I supposed to do?" I ask rubbing the blood from my lip.

"Take the deal, do the time and get on with your life."

She picks up the weed and starts to light it again. "You done ruined my high. Get out of my house."

"I can't go to jail. I have a baby on the way." I blurt.

She laughs, dropping the blunt into her lap. "Got da—boy, get out of my house."

"I'm serious."

"By what fool?"

"Her name is Katrina and she's Ava's friend."

She downs the Jack Daniels in her glass. "You're pitiful."

"I didn't plan this. I only got with Trina to get access to Ava."

"Boy, please. You didn't get with her because of Ava, it's to replace her. We both know you'll latch on to any woman with a house, car, bank account, decent credit, and a pink hole between her legs."

"I love Ava."

"You don't have the capacity to love. You're like your trifling daddy. Whoever he is." She laughs. "You're a user and not a good one either. Lord knows I should have swallowed you as a seed, but no, I had to birth a bobblehead fool. Andre, you got as much sense as a squirrel who doesn't know when to get out of the road. Take the plea deal. As for this other fool, you need to break it to her that you had a vasectomy after you slipped and got the mut pregnant. I don't need her thinking she can depend on me for anything. I don't like kids and I don't have no money."

"You have plenty of money."

"Sho do and sense with it."

"Marble, I think Katrina is stalking Ava. She was watching the news about a house burning down. Ava's house."

"Then I think you need to call the police. Now, get out of my house. Deacon Samuels is coming over and we got plans to do some nasty thangs later."

I look at her, shaking my head.

Getting home, I walk into the bedroom to Katrina sitting in the dark.

I flip on the light. "Before you start, I'm not in the mood."

"Why didn't you answer my calls? I ran out of gas today."

"Oh." I reply going into the closet.

"Is that all you're going to say? I'm the mother of your only child and you can't even pick up the phone when I call?"

"Being pregnant doesn't entitle you to my every move."

"Where you with her?" she asks. "Is that what happened to your lip?"

"Yes. Is this what you want to hear? Yes, I was with her." He puts in air quotes. "Do you hear how stupid you sound? I'm going to take a shower. Either lose the attitude or get out."

"You're not going to acknowledge my hair?"

"You want me to recognize you for combing your hair after accusing me of cheating?"

"I do." She states.

"You need help."

"No. I need you." She yells as I slam the door.

chapter fifteen
Ava

I'm sitting inside of my new truck. A 2022 Kia Telluride SX, dark moss color with butterscotch leather trim, all the bells and whistles and thirty-three miles. I decided to keep my old truck, parking it in a storage facility until I can find a house. I also decided to get a new phone number the other day. I realized the only way to start over is to do so completely.

Pressing June's number, her voice fills the cabin of the truck.

"I hope you're on the way to take me for a ride."

I chuckle. "Not yet. There's a house I want to look at first. I can't sit around moping when I need somewhere else to stay. I have to get on with my life."

"You know our home is always open for you."

"I do, but I can't stay with you guys forever. Besides, you'll spend the time taking care of me when it's you who needs the rest. So, I'm about to see a house in Nesbit, Mississippi then I'm coming to pick you up."

"Nesbit? Dang sis. I'll have to pack a lunch to see you." She giggles.

"You won't. It's only about a thirty-minute drive."

"Oh okay then carry on, but make sure it has a room for me."

"I wouldn't purchase it otherwise. I'll see you in a bit."

"Be safe and I love you."

"I love you too."

———————————

"Good afternoon. My, aren't you pretty." The older woman says when I walk inside. "Is this your first time touring the model home?"

"Thank you and yes ma'am."

"Well come on in and let me give you a tour. We have over six floor plans to choose from. Is there a certain number of rooms you need?"

"Minimum of four."

"Our largest floor plan is the one you're standing in now. It's right at thirty-one hundred square feet with four bedrooms and three baths. Of course, this one is all dolled up with the most expensive upgrades."

"What's the total cost of this one?"

"Um, this one might be out of your price range." She states flipping through paper. "It's a little over four hundred thousand."

"How could it be out of my price range when you don't even know what my price range is? Isn't that being presumptuous?"

Her face turns red.

"I only meant, well, you said, I apologize if that sounded judgmental." She stumbles over her words.

"It didn't sound like it, it was. Tell me, um," I lean in to look at her name tag, "Rose. Do you assume what all your clients can afford or only those who look like me?"

"I'm not a racist." She folds her arm.

"I didn't call you racist, ma'am but the line is ringing. Nevertheless, do you get commission when a house sells in this subdivision?"

"Of course. I'm the listing agent."

"Cool. Are you the only listing agent for this subdivision?"

"At the moment."

"Then, I'd rather buy wood, nails and a hammer from Home Depot to build a shed in the back of my best friend's house before purchasing anything you'll prosper from. Have a great day, Rosie."

"It's Rose." She yells to my back.

Driving a little further down, I stop at the next model home.

"Good afternoon. My name is Lakita Spate, welcome home to Hawthorne Estates."

"Hi, I'm Ava." I take her hand.

"Hi Ava. Come on in."

"Were you headed out?" I inquire seeing her things packed up.

"Yes, but I'm in no hurry. Tell me what you're looking for in a home."

"First, are you the listing agent who'll get commission if I buy?"

"Yes ma'am."

"Good. After leaving Southwood Lake, I'd never buy from them."

"I take it you've met Rose?"

I nod.

"We've received a few clients due to her."

"She should never be the front face of any company. Anyway, I'm not giving her anymore good energy. Lakita, I'm looking for four bedrooms, at least three baths with a nice kitchen, pantry and entertaining backyard preferably with a screened in porch."

"Yass, for knowing what you want." She beams. "In fact, I think I have something you might be interested in."

She pulls up pictures on her computer attached to a TV on the wall. "This one is four bedrooms, three baths and almost thirty-five hundred square feet. The porch isn't screened in, but it can be added. The kitchen will have all the appliances included along with a butler's pantry and coffee nook. This is the backyard. The original plan includes a pool, but it can be redesigned."

"No, I love it. How long is the building process?"

"Usually six months. However, this one is already in the building phase. It was halfway complete when the original buyer pulled out after her husband was killed in a motorcycle accident which means, it can probably be complete by February."

"Oh, I'm sorry to hear that."

"I was too. He was a really nice guy and looking forward to retiring here with his wife of thirty-two years. After his passing, she couldn't bring herself to finish it, so the builder decided to complete the project and put it on the market. Which now presents as a blessing for you. You can negotiate on the price."

"Is it on this street?"

"Yes." She points directly across. "If you have time, we can go through it."

"Are you sure? I don't want to keep you." I tell her.

"Girl, ain't nobody waiting on me but my cat, Tiffy." She laughs. "Follow me."

"Wow." I express walking in.

"They spared no detail." She tells me.

"I can see that. The pictures don't do this justice. I'm only surprised it hasn't sold yet."

"We've had a few inquiries but no offers as of today. If I may ask, are you currently working with a finance company or have you gotten a preapproval?"

"I'm not and no. I plan to pay in cash." I tell her.

"That's what I'm talking about." She gives me a fist bump. "Sorry, if that wasn't professional, but I love to see a black woman doing her thang."

"Me too." I laugh walking into the master bedroom. "Ms. Lakita, I want this house."

"Then let's get you what you want."

chapter sixteen

The following week, I'm back in the office. On Friday, Danny stops by to drop off some of the carrying cases for the Buddi USB. Opening one, I squeal before rushing into Levar's office. "Oh my God. These came out perfect."

He laughs. "I told Danny you would love that one."

"From the colors to the size, they came out much better than I expected."

"I agree. I think we're going to have a hard time keeping them on the shelf. Thank you for your help."

"Um, it's my job sir."

Speaking of, I know you've been out of the office the past two weeks, but have you had a chance to meet with Felecia to go over the job posting for your department?"

"No, and I apologize. I hope it hasn't put things behind."

"Ava, don't you dare apologize for needing time after your home burned down. How are you, by the way? I wanted to reach out but didn't want to overstep."

"You can never overstep." I smile. "To answer your question, I'm refusing to be anything other than better. Frankly, I'm tired of being tired."

"Tired can do one of two things. Push you to fight or give up."

"Giving up is no longer an option for me, not when I have a niece whose mom is fighting to get her here healthy, a fulfilling career, the possibility of a new house and soon a life free of Andre and Katrina."

"Hold on. Not to overshadow all you said, but did you slide in the fact you're buying a house and June is having a baby like it's not a big deal?"

"I did."

"Ava, that's great news. Give me details."

"First, June and Grant have been trying to have a baby the last three years. This is the first pregnancy without complications, and she's made it to five months. Secondly, I put in an offer for a house, praying if it's for me God will allow it. It's brand new and beautiful." I open my phone, going around his desk. "It has a huge kitchen, butler's pantry, coffee nook and I'll be the first to live in it."

"It's beautiful Ava. Congratulations. God is somebody, isn't He?"

"He definitely is." I beam.

"I only have one question. Can you cook?"

"Can I cook? Boy, I can throw down in the kitchen."

"Girl, I'm not talking about chicken alfredo. I'm a manly man who loves pinto beans, cornbread, corn, and fried chicken type of throwing down."

"Am I supposed to be scared?"

"Oh okay, Chef Ava. Prove it."

"Nye, you know I'm living in a hotel." I side eye him.

He leans back in the chair. "I have a kitchen. That's if you're up for the challenge."

"What do I get if I win?"

"Whatever you want?" he replies. "If you lose, it's whatever I want. Deal?" he holds out his hand.

"Nope. I need specifics." I counter. "If I win, I want um a night of dancing."

"Okay." He smiles. "Well, if I win, I want you."

My face heats up and my mouth opens.

"I'm sorry." He stands. "I shouldn't have said that. If I win, you'll have to give me one entire Sunday of uninterrupted time to do whatever I plan."

"Deal. I'll be at your house Sunday morning to drop off what I need."

"You don't even have the address."

"You'll text it." I stop at the door. "By the way, you gave up too easy even though you're going to lose."

He smiles, dropping his head.

After meeting with Felecia to work out the job posting for my department, I pack up to leave. In the truck, I'm singing with the radio when I see blue flashing lights behind me. Pulling over, I let the window down and place my hands on the steering wheel.

"License and registration."

"Officer, can you tell me why I was pulled over?"

"You were speeding. License and registration."

"I'm taking my hands from the steering wheel to reach into my purse for the license and glove box for the registration."

He snatches them from me sliding it in his front pocket. "Have you been smoking weed?"

"Smoking weed? No, I don't smoke and there is no smell coming from my truck."

"Step out of the truck." He orders.

"Why? What have I done that requires getting out officer?"

"Get out of the truck Ava."

"How do you know my name?"

"Out of the truck."

"I'd like a supervisor along with your name, badge number and id card, please."

I reach for my phone.

He pulls his weapon. "Let me see your hands."

"Oh my God. Please don't kill me. I was getting my phone."

He pulls on the handle. "Unlock the door." He yells.

"Sir, I'm not moving while you have that gun trained on me. I asked for a supervisor which is my right. You have my license and registration, please write my ticket and get your supervisor, now."

He slowly backs away from the truck. I quickly get my phone and call Josiah.

"Josiah, I was pulled over by a police officer who says I was speeding, which I wasn't. He ordered me out the car and I refused. I know I shouldn't have, but he seems fishy. I reached for my phone, and he pulled his gun." I nervously tell him without taking a breath. "I'm scared."

"Where are you?"

"On Getwell, right after crossing into Memphis."

"Where's the officer now?"

"He walked back to his car. I asked for a supervisor and his credentials." I look through the mirror. "He's on the phone."

"Hold on."

I raise the phone and take a few pictures of him. When I see him walking back, I lay the phone in my lap, returning my hands to the steering wheel. He comes up, throws my license and registration inside.

"If I were you, I'd be careful." He warns and walks off.

I exhale, quickly rolling the window up.

"Ava, you there?" Josiah asks.

"Yes, he's gone." I tell him. "Did you hear what he said?"

"Yes. Are you okay to come here to file an official report?"

"Yes." I loudly sigh. "He really scared me. He knew my name without looking at my information. Josiah, I have a new truck. How would he know that?"

"I don't know and I'm sorry you've had to experience this. However, I will ensure we get to the bottom of this. I'm sending you the address. Call when you're here and I'll have someone meet you downstairs."

chapter seventeen
Katrina

"Stop calling me." I scream into the phone, bumping into my coworker Barbara.

"Is that woman continually harassing you?" she asks.

"Yes, and it's driving me crazy."

"Didn't you file paperwork for the order of protection?"

"Yeah, but they have to serve her."

"Then call your attorney. The stress isn't good for the baby. There should be something the law can do and if you need me as a witness, let me know."

"Thanks Barbara. I appreciate it."

I smile walking out the door. Pulling up to Andre's house, I see him standing outside talking to another woman. I park in the driveway and get out.

"Andre." I call out and he holds up his hand.

"No, he didn't." I state putting my bags on the trunk and joining them.

They continue to talk like I'm not standing there. "Hello, my name is Katrina, Andre's fiancé and mother of his child. You are?"

She looks at me. "Someone who doesn't care. D, I'll call you."

She gets into her car and drives off.

"What the hell was that?" he angrily asks snatching my arm.

"You wouldn't introduce me." I snatch away.

"Introduce you for what? That conversation had nothing to do with you."

"Really? You're talking to some random woman who has her hand all over you and expect me to say nothing."

"Yes, it would have been the best thing."

"Who was she?"

He goes into the house.

"Who was she D?" I mock the name she used following him inside. "Are you cheating on me with some random slut while I'm carrying your baby?"

"Katrina, back off."

"Or what?"

He glares at me.

"Tell me who she is?"

"Her name is Christina." He yells. "We used to work together."

"Why was she here?"

"I don't owe you an explanation."

I pick up a picture frame from the bookcase and throw it at him.

"Are you crazy?"

"I sure am and if I was you, I wouldn't take my kindness for weakness. I'm going to ask you again. Who was she?" I scream.

"She used to be a jailer who lost her job for letting me use her phone the night I was arrested and I'm trying to help her."

"Help her how?"

"With getting her job back. Now, are you done interrogating me, Detective Dummy?"

"For the time being and I got your dummy sweetie. You better recognize, I'm not Ava. I won't roll over for you."

He chuckles. "When you're done with whatever this is, leave. I'm not in the mood to pacify you and your feelings tonight. I have enough to worry about without adding your insecurities to the list. Let yourself out."

He goes into the bedroom, slamming the door.

"Oh no. You're not going to dismiss me. Bring your ass out of there and talk to me. Andre, do you hear me?" I go over pounding and kicking on the door. When that doesn't work, I cry out in pain. "Owww. Andre." I whine. "Andre, I need your help."

He opens the door to find me hunched over.

"I think there's something wrong with the baby."

"Then you need a doctor. Find one on your way home."

He steps around me and I stand straight. A few seconds later, I rush behind him into the living room.

"You'd really leave me in pain?" I push him. "What if something was really wrong?"

"Katrina, take your ass on."

"Or what? Are you going to choke me?"

He steps back. "Be gone when I return, or you'll find out."

"Where are you going? Andre." I scream to the top of my lungs.

Andre

Leaving there, I drive by Ava's house. Stopping when I see it boarded up, I get out the car. I try her number although I know she has me blocked. I pull the phone away when I hear the message, *'the number you dialed is not a working number.'*

Dropping the phone into the cupholder, I head to McCluster's bar, a small hole in the wall frequented by police.

"What's up Powell? I ain't seen you in a while." Roger states.

"Man, a whole lot of drama." I tell him taking a seat.

"You having your usual?"

"Doubled."

"Man, you still got woman problems?"

"More like women." I sip the Bourbon.

"Sucks to be you."

When he walks away, I decline Katrina's call before dialing Clay's number.

"Hey man. No, I'm at McCluster's and I need your help. I'll be here."

Thirty minutes later, I meet Clay outside.

"What's up dude? Your ball & chain let you out on a weekday?" he jokes.

"Man, I'm not married."

"Does she know that?"

"Forget Katrina. I need you to find Ava for me."

"No way. I'm not getting in the middle of whatever y'all got going."

"I wouldn't ask if it wasn't important. Her house burned downed, and I didn't know how bad until I went there. Bro, I'm worried Katrina may have done something to her. Can you at least call her?"

"No."

"Then what about her friend June. I only want to know she's okay. Will you at least call her?"

"Fine, but if this comes back—

"It won't."

"What's June's number?"

"I don't have it. Can't you look it up?"

"Dude. You were with Ava all this time and you don't have her best friend's number?"

"You know your wife's best friend?"

"Her best friend, sisters, and mother. If anybody knows my wife better than me, it's them. What's June's last name?"

My forehead creases.

"Man. I'm getting a drink."

I spend the next hour destroying my liver with alcohol before heading home, breathing a sigh of relief when I don't see Katrina's car. However, the joy is short lived when I walk in to see she'd destroyed my living room.

"This bit—damn it." I yell.

In the midst of cleaning up, my phone dings with a message from an unknown number.

1 (901) 777-0900: You didn't get this from me.

chapter eighteen

Hours later, I walk into the lobby of the hotel, still upset about the supposed traffic stop. My steps halt at the sight of Andre standing in the lobby.

"I come in peace." He says coming towards me with his hands up.

"You don't even know the meaning of the word. How did you know I was here?" I ask.

"Ava, I'll always be able to find you."

"Yeah, you made that obvious by sending your flunky to intimidate me. Well, I'm serving you notice, it will not work. See, I've had all I'm going to take from you and your baby momma, Fruit Cake Katrina and if you think I'm going to shrink into a corner and let y'all have any more of my peace, think again." I poke him in the chest. "Sir, let this serve as the final notice. I'm going to fight you, her and if need be, the Memphis Police with everything in me. The scared Ava is gone."

"Ava, maybe you need to start listening. I don't have to send anyone to intimidate you. Besides, I don't work for Memphis Police anymore. You made sure of that."

"No, you did when you wrapped your hands around my throat. God." I yell. "When will you take responsibility for your actions?"

He grabs my hand. "I have which is why I'm here. I realize I've made a lot of mistakes regarding you. I talked to my mom and—

"Marble?" I snatch away laughing. "Man, she's the last person you should be listening too. Hell, she's partly to blame for the way you are and until you truly deal with your mommy issues, you'll continually find yourself realizing things too late." I press the button for the elevator.

"Ma'am is everything okay?" a hotel worker inquires.

"Yes sir. He's leaving."

"Ava, all I want is another chance."

"You'll have that with somebody else." I step into the elevator. "When you're released from prison."

He jumps into the elevator before the door closes.

"Andre don't touch me. It's obvious you're drunk."

"I'm not going to hurt you. I wanted to make sure you were okay."

"You are hurting me." I correct. "Every time you do this, you're hurting me. Not leaving me alone is hurting me. Sending your baby momma and friends for me is hurting me. I've lost so much fooling with you and sad reality, I'm still losing. Please. For the last time, leave me alone."

When the elevator dings on my floor, he shrinks into the corner, and I get off. Rushing to the door, I quickly use my phone to unlock it. Pressing my back against it, letting my purse and bag slide from arm.

"Oh Lord, I need a touch from You. I really need a touch from You." I begin to sing a remix of Tamela Mann's song. "No other one will ever do. Oh Lord, I need a touch from you. I really need a touch from you. Ugh." I scream.

The vibration of my watch pulls me from the moment. I raise my arm to see a text from June.

Are you okay?

I inhale and exhale, picking up my bags and feelings to reply.

An hour later, I'm online booking an Airbnb. Thankfully, there's one close to the job I can move into tomorrow.

My phone rings with a Facetime call from Levar.

"Hey, are you okay?"

"I will be." I reply sliding under the covers to talk to him.

———

Sunday morning, I roll over to silence the alarm on my phone and see a text from Levar.

Levar: Hey, my apologies for texting so late, but I have an early meeting and won't be back in time to let you in the house in the morning. However, the code to the garage is 09900. The alarm code is 0990. Let yourself in. I'll be back by 5 in time for dinner with a big appetite. <smiling emoji>

Me: And ready to accept this L, sir.

Hours later, after organizing my things at the Airbnb, I let myself into Levar's house.

"Okay, Mr. Wilson." I gush walking inside, punching the code to disarm the alarm and putting my purse on the island. I take a quick tour of the downstairs, gazing at the pictures on his mantle before returning to the truck for my other items. Inside the kitchen, I go over to the Bluetooth radio on the wall, connecting it to my phone. Shuffling my Sunday's playlist, *Amazing Grace* by Kathy Taylor plays.

I look through the cabinets until I find the pots, pans, and a pitcher. I start by cleaning the beans and putting them in water to soak before washing out the dishes. I fill the pot with water and chicken stock adding onion, ham hocks, and seasoning. Placing it on the stove and turning on the heat. Once it's boiling, I turn down the fire and go about cutting up the chicken. Once it's seasoned, I prep the corn, batter for the cornbread and items for a butter roll then make a pitcher of Kool-Aid. Afterwards, I add the beans to the pot and cover it.

With everything prepped, I take a step back to admire my work. Growing up in foster homes and barely being fed, I was determined to never depend on anyone else to feed me. So, I taught myself to cook. It took a lot of trial and error, yet I can hold my own. After cleaning up and turning off the music, I go into the living room.

Thank God he has a TV I can work.

"Okay charging station." I mumble, laying my phone on it.

Clicking on the Facebook Watch app, I start to search for June's church service when my phone rings. I slide the bar, pressing the speaker button.

"Hello."

"Ava, hi this is Pastor Hunter, did I catch you at a bad time?"

"No sir."

"First and foremost, please forgive me for not calling before now. Truth is, I shouldn't have allowed you to leave after the meeting and God has been dealing with me. This morning while in preparation for service, I couldn't go another minute without calling to make amends. Ava, I will not beat around the bush, we were wrong and on behalf of Lady Hunter and the deacon board, I offer you our sincerest apology."

I sigh. "Pastor Hunter, I appreciate you calling and for the apology. I was blindsided, confused, and most of all hurt. However, I forgive you all and pray better guidelines will be set when confronting members on any matter."

"You're right and we've already begun the process by sending all of our leadership to classes on dealing with conflict resolution, the value of the tongue and more. We never want to hurt another person the way we did you. Ava, I won't hold you and thank you for taking my call. I hope, in the present, you'll give us another opportunity to serve you spiritually."

"Honestly, I haven't decided if I'll return as a member, but I'm leaving the decision up to God. In the meantime, I wish you all the best. Take care Pastor Hunter."

"You too Ava."

I end the call, closing my eyes to pray. "God, lead me where you'll have me. Don't allow my feelings to blind me from seeing you in every situation and circumstance. And Father, I do forgive them and pray their countenance will be forever changed. Amen."

Picking up the remote, I click on the first live worship service.

"Isn't it amazing the many ways God will try to get our attention when we're doing the very thing that goes against His will for us? God tried three times to stop Balaam, but he was too blinded by sin to see Him. Being in sin, darkness, and wickedness does that. It'll have us unable to see God and turning on those who'd never let us down. This is why God asks Balaam in verse 32, "*Why have you struck your donkey these three times? Behold, I have come out to stand against you, because your way is perverse before Me.*" Perverse Biblically means to or be precipitate, push headlong, or drive recklessly. Precipitate means done, made, or acting suddenly or without careful consideration.

Here, the angel of the Lord is trying to stop Balaam from harming himself and he can't see it. Now, don't be quick to judge Balaam when we've been there too. Baby, some of us will break traffic laws and lie to momma to get to sin, caring about nothing else since sin changes our heart, even momentarily. Sin is intoxicating and iniquity perverts our mind causing us to do evil in the eyesight of God. Yet, even when we've made God our adversary, He'll send a delay to spare our lives, if we're willing to see it.

Church, let me ask you a question. What if the thing you lost is God making space for something bigger and better? What if the delay is God's saving you from making another mistake or bad choice you don't have the strength not to make? What if God delays the punishment you deserve to give you time to come to your senses? What if God is saving you from you. Biblically, a female donkey is called a she-ass. In this passage, verse 27 says, *"And when the ass saw the angel of the LORD, she fell down under Balaam."* Let me ask it this way. What if falling on your ass saved you?

Some of us ought to be praying, "God, thank you for stopping me from chasing what has the power to crush me. Thank you for standing in my way when I was headed to revive what you've been telling me to let die. God, thank you for standing in my way when I couldn't see it was me causing the problem. God, thank you for standing in my way, freeing me from inflicting the wounds. God, thank you for standing in my way. Your standing saved me."

"God, thank you for standing in my way. Your standing saved me." I repeat yawning.

My eyes open when something nudges me.

"Um, who are you?" the chick standing over me asks.

I quickly sit up.

"I'm Ava. Who are you?"

"I'm Levitra, Levar's wife. Why are you in my house?"

chapter nineteen

I press power on the remote to stop the video playing and stand.

"I'm sorry, you're who?"

She looks me up and down before laughing.

"It was a joke. Hi, I'm Levar's baby sister."

I sit back on the couch.

"Girl, I thought I was going to have to fight on this good Sunday morning." I tell her.

"My bad. I thought it would be funny."

"Definitely not funny, but it's nice to meet you."

"Please don't tell my brother or he might revoke my key privileges. I only came to get some supplies I keep in the basement."

I smile, looking at my watch to see it's after two. I rush into the kitchen to check on my beans. Removing the top, I wash my hands and get a spoon. Breathing a sigh of relief they didn't burn.

A few minutes later, Levitra comes in. "It smells good in here."

"Thank you."

"I'm really sorry about waking you and for what I said."

"It's no problem. Although the joke was bad," I smile, "I needed to be up before my beans burned. I would have never lived that down with your brother."

"True. He's very competitive."

"We have that in common, hence my reason for being here." I reply turning the oven on and pulling the other items from the refrigerator.

"What are you cooking?" she asks as her watch dings.

"Chicken, pinto beans, fried corn, cornbread, okra and a butter roll. Oh, and Kool-Aid."

"Okay, I'm with it. You're pulling out all the stops. Please save me a plate. FYI, my mother, and I are rooting for you."

She grabs her things and leave without giving me a chance to ask what she means.

Shrugging it off, I finish the butter roll, placing it in the oven.

Sometime later, I'm dancing and singing to the Blues song *Too Long* by King George while taking the cornbread out the oven.

"But I found me a good thang and I don't care what they say. I gotta keep moving. My man, he waiting—oh my God." I jump at the sight of Levar leaning against the entrance to the kitchen.

"I can get used to this." He smiles walking closer to me.

"What?"

"Coming home to you, a gorgeous, black, educated, cooking, dancing and sanging woman."

"You don't even know if I can cook yet." I joke, hoping my cheeks haven't turned red from blushing.

"True, but I'll have you. How are you?" he questions wrapping his arms around me.

"Better now." I hug him back. "How are you?"

He pulls back to look at me. "Do you even have to ask? I'm going to freshen up before I get fresh in this kitchen." He pecks me on the lips, turning to walk away.

I stand there for a second, smiling and touching my lips.

"Get it together Ava."

Thirty minutes later, he comes in after showering and changing clothes. I switched to R&B on my Pandora station and turned the music down.

"What can I do?"

"You can grab the pitcher from the refrigerator and glasses."

He pulls the refrigerator door open and stands there. "Ava Justine Gentry, I know you didn't make Kool-Aid?"

"Did you call my whole name?"

"Girl, unuh, hold up." He rushes to the cabinet, gets a glass adding ice before filling it up. "And it's made with diabetical love. That's it." He places the glass on the table. "Get your shoes."

"Where are we going?"

"To the courthouse."

"Boy, if you don't get back here so we can eat." I laugh. "Besides, it's Sunday."

"Shoot." He snaps his fingers. "Guess, I'll have to wait."

I shake my head and go about fixing our plates, sitting his in front of him. I go back and get the bowls of beans. Once I'm seated, he takes my hand and says grace.

"I put the beans in a bowl. I like a little of the juice with mine. Feel free to add them to your plate."

"No, this is perfect, and it's call pot liquor."

"I know what it's called, country."

He smiles crumbling some of his cornbread on top of them before adding onions. Inserting a spoonful into his mouth, his eyes close. "Okay, okay we working with something."

I roll my eyes. "Hush and eat."

The room is silent, except for Levar's smacking and moaning.

"How is it?" I inquire when he puts the bowl up to his lips.

He looks over the top. "Where do you want to go dancing?"

I wiggle in my chair.

"I don't know why you asked. You know this food is fye, although I may need a bottle of Gas-x later." He says getting up for more.

I chuckle. "There's some on the counter."

He turns back to look at me and I shrug.

"How was your meeting?"

"It was good. Michael and I met with some manufacturing executives to see about placing Buddi and accessories in stores."

"That's great news."

"Yes, and the feedback was positive. Prayerfully, we'll have the approvals before we officially launch in February."

"I have no doubt you will."

"Enough of business, tell me more about Ava."

"Well, you know mostly all there is." I go on to tell him a little of my childhood, education and how I met Andre.

"Is that how you got the scar?"

My hand instinctively touches it. "Yeah. I couldn't afford the best of care, at the time, so I was left with this ugly mark. Thank God it's not as noticeable as it used to be."

"It's only ugly if it doesn't remind you of what you've survived."

"Amen. Oh, speaking of ugly, your sister stopped by."

"Wait, did you call my sister ugly?"

I spit a little of the Kool-Aid out laughing. "I didn't mean it like that. Oh my God." I continue laughing as he joins in. I dab my mouth with the napkin. "I'm sorry. What I meant was, she fooled me with an ugly joke."

"Oh Lord. What did she do?"

"I'd fallen asleep on the couch. She woke me up saying she was your wife."

He puts his head in his hand. "That girl."

"She apologized and asked me not to tell you, so you can't say anything." I tell him standing to clean up.

"Yeah, not happening."

"Go easy on her. So, how'd I do?"

"Wellll," he drags out. "Baby, that food was slamming. Don't tell my momma, but you up there with them old ladies from the church kitchen on Sunday. How did you learn to cook like that?"

"Watching videos, reading blogs, and having a determination to never go hungry. Speaking of your mom, your sister said something I wanted to ask you about."

"What's that?"

"She said she and your mom are rooting for me. What does that mean?"

"I may talk about you a little and they, like me, want you to survive this season of your life. I also told them about the bet."

"I hope you're ready to tell them I won."

"You definitely won. I'm stuffed."

"Too stuffed for dessert?"

"Dessert?" he excitedly asks as I place butter roll on two small plates.

"Butter roll?" he squeals. "Ava, I only have one question left."

"What's that?"

"Spend the night with me."

chapter twenty

"Mr. Wilson, are you calling me easy?" I question.

"Of course not. Although I asked the right thing, I didn't mean it in a sexual nature. Here's the truth." He stands taking the plates, sitting them on the counter and grabbing my hands. "I like you, a lot. I've liked you since I met you at the restaurant and you may not believe this, but you're my good thing and I'm favored more by you being in my life."

"How could you know that?" I ask with hesitation.

"I prayed and asked God for your heart before we ever met. Ava, I prayed for the ability to love my wife like she deserves. I prayed for patience to wait on you, for wisdom to understand what you've endured, for hands to pull you from the darkness of your yesterday and a mouth to speak life into you. I prayed and prepared to be your strength, the head of your life, help mate, husband, father of your children, loudest cheerleader, prayer partner, comforter, and lover."

He wipes the tears falling from my eyes.

"One day soon, I'm going to stand before our family and friends, under the anointing of God reciting vows I don't plan to break. I'll tell them how God created you for me and no matter what we've each experienced, or how long it has taken us to find one another, it hasn't tainted the plans God has for us. All of it brought us to this moment and when you'll have me, I promise—

"Stop." I interrupt. "Please." I step away from him. "Don't make promises."

"Ava, I won't apologize for wanting to love you. Yes, I know people have let you down in the past, but don't make me pay for their mistakes."

"That's not what I'm doing. Levar, I want, no I desire the kind of love you're professing. God knows, I've waited my entire life for it, and I don't want to mess it up with my insecurities of the past. When I say don't make promises, I mean from the standpoint they can be broken, even if you never intend too. Therefore, show me with your actions. Levar, all the love I've ever experienced has been painful and right now, I'm healing those wounds to keep from bleeding on you. I'm healing in order to accept your love, not abuse it. I'm healing so when I stand before God, our family and friends to recite vows, they're with the man only death will separate me from."

"You said ours." He smiles, stepping closer. I move back until I'm pressed against the refrigerator. "Ava, I'm not perfect and I will make mistakes along the way, but

I'll never intentionally hurt you. Yet, I won't apologize for what the past has done. What I will do is show you who Levar Tyrell Wilson is cause my daddy didn't raise no boy."

I look off.

"Look at me babe. Will you let me in?"

"I'm scared." I whisper.

He kisses my forehead. "I'll wait."

When he begins to move, I grab his arm. "But I'm ready."

He blinks his eyes, grabbing my face with both hands. "Say it again."

"I'm ready for you love me."

"One more time."

"I said I'm ready to let you in and give you me."

He begins planting kisses all over my face before picking me up causing me to squeal.

"Hold on." I tell him. "I am going to do a background check on you."

"Good since I've already done one on you." He winks referring to the job.

The next morning, I wake up and it takes a minute to remember I spent the night at Levar's. After cleaning up the kitchen and storing the leftovers, we stayed up talking and listening to music. I filled him in on the latest

Andre and Katrina saga and me moving. I didn't want him blindsided by anything. It was around three when he offered me the guestroom. I roll over on my back, smiling.

You don't even love yourself. How can you expect someone else too?

I hear Andre's voice causing me to sit straight up.

"Devil and flesh, you're a liar. I may have gotten it wrong before, but I'm no longer allowing my flesh, self-doubt, unhealed wounds and what almost destroyed me to take away the good I deserve. God, I come out of agreement with fear and replace it with the sound of obedience to your will for my life. Close my ears to the voice of the enemy and the past, letting me hear you. Let my eyes see beyond the natural and allow my heart to love.

God, thank you. Thank you for not giving up on me and letting me give up on myself. Oh and God, thank you for fine, educated, professional, home owning, business minded, good smelling man who waited for me. Thank you for upgrading my palette to know what real love taste like. Prepare my mind, body, and soul to complement, and not hinder his life. I love you Lord and I trust you. Amen."

Changing out of Levar's t-shirt, I redress in what I had on yesterday and make up the bed. Going into the bathroom, I find a new toothbrush, toothpaste, and towels in the closet. Once done, I grab my things.

"Good morning. How'd you sleep?" Levar asks when I walk into the kitchen.

"Amazingly. That mattress is the bomb."

"You're welcome to it any time." He smiles. "You want coffee?"

"No, I'm going to head to the house and shower before I'm late for work. I wouldn't want the boss to write me up."

"I think you'll get a pass." He pulls me into a kiss. "Thank you."

"For what?"

"Dinner, this, and the prayer this morning."

"You heard that, huh?"

"I did. You think I'm fine?"

"Is that all you heard?" I laugh.

He shuts me up with a passionate kiss before walking me out.

"Be safe and I'll see you shortly."

chapter twenty-one
Josiah

I motion for the officer to come in.

"Lieutenant, you wanted to see me?" he stops short when he sees Deputy Chief of Uniform Patrol Samuel Oakley and Internal Affairs Rep, Walt Riesling.

"Have a seat."

After making the introductions of those in the room, Riesling begins to question Officer Miguel Suarez.

"Officer Suarez, were you on duty Friday around 17:30 hours?"

"No sir."

"Were you in a department issued vehicle on Friday around 17:30 hours?"

"Yes sir. Headed home."

"Where's home?"

"Whitehaven." He answers.

"What is your district and precinct?"

"District one and Raines."

"Does your patrol route cover the Getwell and Holmes area?"

"No sir." He nervously answers.

"Would you like to tell us why you pulled over a citizen for a traffic stop in that area while you were off duty and out of jurisdiction?"

"I, uh—

"Please think carefully before you answer Officer Suarez."

"Is this an administrative inquiry and am I under orders to respond?" he sits up in the chair.

"This is an internal investigation, and you are thereby ordered to answer."

"Then I'd like to have a representative present before I answer any more questions." He states.

"No problem." IA Rep Riesling replies. "You are hereby suspended pending the outcome of the investigation of official misconduct, harassment, the unauthorized operation of a department vehicle and refusal to answer all pertinent questions relevant to an investigation. Please turn in your badge, gun, and identification. You'll also need to leave the patrol car."

He stands, lays everything on the desk then leaves.

"Lieutenant Rainey, we'll be in touch once we've had time to investigate." Riesling assures me.

I go about finishing the paperwork when my cell phone rings.

"This is Josiah Rainey. Yes. Okay." I listen to Fire Investigator Kevin Mason explain the outcome of their investigation. The deceased was Eddie Wagner, and the fire has been deemed an accident. Apparently, his wife kicked him out and she had no idea where he'd gone. From Mr. Warren's cell phone records, Eddie tried to call him a few times before going to his house, but he never received the calls. "Thanks for letting me know. I appreciate the work you all have put in."

I hang up, call Naomi, filling her in and asking her to call Mr. Warren.

A knock on the door.

"Come in."

"Lieutenant, this was dropped off for you." Kim says handing me an envelope.

"Thanks. Do you know who it's from?"

"No sir. A messenger delivered it."

She leaves and I open it. Pictures of Ava and Andre fall onto the desk.

You're protecting a liar.

Looking through the pictures, I see one of Andre holding her hand and another of him getting into the elevator. I drop them and dial her number.

"Good morning, Josiah." She chipperly answers. "How are you?"

"Good morning. I'm good. You?"

"Great. Headed to work."

"I won't hold you, but I heard from the Fire Investigator and the body was that of Mr. Warren's friend Eddie, therefore the fire has been labeled an accident."

"Lord." She sighs. "Although I'm saddened by the loss of life, a part of me is relieved it wasn't Andre or Katrina."

"Speaking of. I received a package this morning of photos."

"Photos of who?"

"You and Andre. Ava, I have to ask. Are you back with him?"

"God no." She bellows. "Josiah, I'm not sure what kind of pictures you received, but there's a better chance of Tina getting back with Ike before I'd ever give Andre access to me again."

"They look to be at a hotel. He's holding your hand and another one shows him getting in the elevator."

"He was waiting at the hotel the other night after I met with you. However, those pictures are misleading. You can check the cameras and see, he never got off with me. Wait. You don't think he set this up, do you?"

"It's possible and judging from the note whoever sent them is angry at you."

"What does it say?" she inquires.

"You're protecting a liar." I read and she chuckles.

"Man, I'm so sick of having to defend and explain myself. Josiah, I can assure you, it isn't what it looks like. Sir, I'd rather sweep all of downtown with a toothbrush and paper made dustman rather than take him back."

"Ava, I'm not judging you. I'll only say this, be careful. Oh, there's an open investigation against Officer Suarez whose been placed on suspension. You should be hearing from someone in Internal Affairs soon."

"Thank you and I apologize for continually dragging you and Naomi into my mess."

"You don't owe us an apology. We're family now, Ava. Talk to you soon. Have a great day." I tell her.

"You as well. Give Naomi my love. Wait Josiah. Speaking of Andre, I never want to make the mistakes I did with him. Can you refer me to someone who can run a background check?"

"Personal?"

"Yes."

"Hmm, I may have someone. I'll text their contact info."

"Thanks."

chapter twenty-two
Ava

Hanging up from Josiah, I grip the steering wheel feeling anger beginning to rise when my phone rings with a call from June.

"Hey sis."

"Don't hey sis me. Why didn't I hear from your tail last night? I was waiting to see how dinner went."

"My bad. It was late and I didn't want to wake you."

"Yeah, yeah. Did you win though?"

"Sis, come on. Of course I won."

"Then why do you sound dry like you've been drinking powder for breakfast? What happened?" she asks.

I fill her in on the conversation with Josiah.

"Screw Joseph and Josephine, AKA Andre and Katrina. We know either one or both are responsible. I knew him popping up was trouble. Ava, listen to me. You're in the midst of God shifting your life and with every shift, the enemy shows up to sift, ensuring you don't make it out of this season with your mind. Yet, like Jesus said to Simon, I'm praying your faith doesn't fail."

"What would I do without you?"

"Thank God you'll never have to find out. Now, back to last night. Tell me one thing, did you make butter roll?"

I laugh. "And did, yet it was my Kool-Aid that had him proposing a shotgun wedding at the courthouse."

"Girl, the Kool-Aid was an added bonus. That man has had stars in his eyes regarding you for the longest. Hence, the Tiffany box for your birthday. My only question, did you accept?"

I don't answer.

"Gul, this ain't the time to hold your peace."

"Kind of." I drag out.

"AJ Gentry, don't make me show up at your job to key that new truck." She hisses. "Spit it out."

"Calm down hormonal Henrietta. No to the proposal and yes to dating."

She squeals.

"Wait, we're happy about this, aren't we?" she clarifies.

"Yes, but I'd be lying if I said I wasn't scared."

"You're doing something new and stepping from behind this wall created to protect you, you're bound to be scared. Nevertheless, don't allow the fear to keep you from seeing happiness."

"I'm trying but am I moving too fast?" I question.

"By who's time? Ava, you deserve happiness and if Levar can give you it, take it. Shoot, there are folks getting married at first sight and finding lasting love. Why can't you?"

I sigh.

"Hear me. Your past may be talking, but you don't have to listen. Yes, we wish there was a pill to erase all we've gone through or a magic potion to catapult us back in time to do things over, yet there isn't. However, it doesn't mean you don't get to be happy. Andre, ole square head tail may have tried to destroy you, but God took the brokenness and refurbished you for the new hands who knows how to appreciate the valuable work of art you are."

"You're right. How will I experience what God has for me if I never try?"

"And since we're saved, here's the King James version, go ye therefore and geteth thou man."

"Geteth—goodbye. I'm pulling up to work. I'll call you later."

I hang up laughing, parking in front of the building. Walking into the office, I sit my things on the desk to start the day. A little later, I'm going through some resumes for a Senior Project Manager when I stop at the very last one.

"This has to be a joke."

I press speaker and Felicia's extension. She doesn't answer. I grab it, heading to her office. Passing Levar's door I hear Felicia's raised voice and my name.

"What about Ava?" he asks.

"How well do you know this chick? Did you even do your research before bringing her on board or are you too blinded by lust? Look at this. There are multiple pages of stuff. Did you know she was fired from her last job for sleeping with her boss and she's involved in a criminal case with her ex? Oh, here's the juiciest piece. She's selling her ass on Only Fans. For Christ's sake Levar. Where did you find her, Craigs List?"

"You're out of line." He tells her. "Ava—

"Ava is right here, and you have a lot of nerve." I say pushing the door open.

"This is a private conversation." Felicia states. "You can wait outside."

"If it was private you should have closed the door. However, I'll leave before I lose my job telling you about yourself."

"I'm listening." She scoffs.

"How dare you stand there badmouthing me over things you know nothing about. As the head of Human Resources, you should know better than to defame a person's character without facts which can lead to lawsuits."

"I've said nothing wrong. It's all right here in black and white."

"Doesn't make it true and had you come to me and asked, you'd know. Although I don't owe you an explanation, allow me to give facts. I was wrongfully terminated which resulted in a winning verdict on my behalf. Furthermore, yes, I'm involved in a criminal case against my ex who tried to kill me. Wouldn't you want to guarantee he goes to jail if you were in my shoes? No need to answer. As for the Only Fans, baby it has taken the majority of my life to love every part of me, and now that I do, I have no desire to sell it to anybody. Fan or not and if you would have taken a good look at those pictures, you'd know it isn't me. However, think and believe what you want, but the next time you want to talk about me, get the full story."

She flips through the pictures. Her eyes widen. "I'm sorry. Levar, I didn't know."

"I'm not the one you need to apologize to." He tells her.

"Ava, I'm sorry for not coming to you, but I will not apologize for looking out for this company. I've come to love Michael and Levar as brothers and don't want to see them taken advantage of."

"How exactly would I have taken advantage of them? Ma'am, they sought me out and I will not stand here trying to justify why when you're the one who handled the background check. No, you overreacted based on what somebody sent you to slander me. I know this because the same pictures were sent to the church. Yet, the thing which truly irks me is the fact, you were quick to believe it over my character."

"Felicia, I need to talk to Ava."

She stops in front of me, but I put my hand up to prevent her from saying anything else.

"Ava, on behalf of Felicia, I apologize. When she burst into my office, I had no idea what it was about. Nonetheless, I don't want you to think I hired you for anything other than the brilliance you bring to Small Sticks. Having you here is a bonus, but it isn't lust and I'd never allow my feelings to overshadow the work you contribute to making this company what it is."

"I never thought there was an ulterior motive in my hiring, but I'm freaking tired of having to explain myself and fight who or what I shouldn't. I had to do the very thing this morning with Josiah. He got pictures too of Andre at my hotel. Levar, every day it's something and this year has taken more out of me than my entire daggum life. I didn't think I'd have to do fight here. I get her wanting to protect you and Michael, however there's a standard of quality of how to handle things, especially being the head of HR."

"You're right. Personal feelings should not be hashed out in the office. No matter what Felicia believed, she handled things the wrong way."

"Oh, she definitely did, yet I'm learning not to hold grudges. Anyway, I was headed to her office to discuss this." I hand him the resume.

"You're kidding. The audacity of this woman." He remarks. "Does she really think we'll hire her?"

"I'm contemplating calling her for an interview to see." I smirk.

"Your choice, but do you really want the negativity associated with it?"

"It would be gratifying to see Penelope's face though."

He walks toward me. "Can I hug you?"

"Really?" I put my hands on my hips.

"The right hug has power. Try it."

I walk into the embrace.

"Take a breath."

"If I do, I may break." I reply.

"Breathe woman."

I inhale then exhale. "I need a safe place."

"Let me be it. Breathe."

I inhale then exhale.

"It's not your responsibility."

"No, it's my choice. Breathe."

I inhale then exhale tightening my hold on him.

He squeezes me. "Do you feel that?"

"Yes."

"Can you breathe?"

"Yes."

"Here, you're safe."

chapter twenty-three

The following Wednesday evening, Levar and I are preparing to leave the office for dinner when I get a call from Lakita with Hawthorne Estates. She and I met to go over my offer for the property before she submitted it, a few weeks ago.

"This is Ava. Hi Lakita. No ma'am. Okay. Really? Oh my God, thank you. Okay. I'll see you then. Merry Christmas."

I turn to see Levar staring.

"I got the house. Oh my God. I have a house. Wow. I'm buying my first house."

He comes over touching my face.

"Say it as many times as you need to let it sink in."

"Babe, I'm buying my first house." I squeal throwing my arms around his neck.

"More for us to celebrate."

Standing out front, I'm texting June while Levar locks up.

"Ava, Ava Gentry."

I turn to see two Southaven and two Memphis police officers. My heart begins to race.

"Are you Ava Gentry?" one of the Memphis officers asks.

"I am. What's this about? Did something happen?"

"We have a warrant for your arrest."

I laugh. "You can't be serious?"

"What's going on?" Levar questions.

"Sir, step back. Ma'am, please place your hands behind your back." One of them demands getting ready to grab me.

"Okay, okay. I'm not resisting, but I'd like to see the warrant."

One of them hands me the paper.

"Stalking and harassing." I shake my head giving it to Levar. "Will you call June and Jamia and take my things?" I ask him while placing my hands behind my back.

"Yeah, and I'm right behind you. Don't worry."

The Miranda rights are stated, and I'm put into the back of the car.

An hour later, I'm sitting inside a cold, gray interrogation room when the door opens. Jamia rushes in followed by two detectives.

"Thank God. Jamia, what is going on?" I ask her.

"Ma'am, my name is Detective David Arias, and this is my partner Detective Scott Hamilton." He goes over the preliminaries and has me sign a document verifying I've been read my rights.

"Ms. Gentry, would you like to speak to us?" Arias asks.

"Couldn't we have done this before I was arrested at my job?"

"We had no way of getting in touch with you."

"Yet, you showed up at my place of employment. Whatever. Can we get this over with?"

"Do you know a Katrina Gaskins?"

"Unfortunately. She's been a pain in my as—side for the last few months."

"According to Ms. Gaskins, she's in fear of her life due in part to you. She states you've been calling, sending emails and texts threatening her life."

"Sir, Katrina isn't valuable enough for me to spend time stalking, harassing nor threatening. She's lying."

"According to these text messages and emails, they prove otherwise." He advises sliding papers over to me. "I'm going to be honest with you. The evidence is pretty convincing."

I laugh. "This doesn't even sound like me. Hoe, I'm going to stomp the bastard child out of your stomach as soon as I lay eyes on you." I read out loud. "Seriously? This lady is sick in the head." I push the papers back. "A.

I have no reason to be upset about this supposed pregnancy. B. If I was, I doggone sure wouldn't text it."

"Why do you think she'd go through all the trouble of filing a false police report so convincing a judge would sign a warrant for your arrest?"

"The same reason shows like Deadly Women and Fatal Vows are popular on the ID channel. A man."

"Andre Powell?" he asks referring to a piece of paper. "What is your relationship with Mr. Powell?"

"He's an ex who tried to kill me." I blatantly answer. "An ex I have no desire to be with and surely wouldn't fight over."

"Are you sure about that?"

He slides over the pictures from the hotel. "Care to explain those? From the looks of it, you and Mr. Powell are quite cozy."

"Sir, I'd rather cuddle with a bear while covered in honey from head to toe than to ever be in a relationship with him."

"My client isn't answering anymore questions. Please send her over to booking so she can be bailed out." Jamia instructs.

"Very well. We'll have an officer come to transfer her to Jail East."

When they leave Jamia turns to me.

"Those same pictures were sent to Josiah." I admit to her. "I'm going to tell you the exact thing I told him. I'm not back with Andre. He was at the hotel when I walked in from filing the complaint on the officer. He jumped in the elevator, but he did not get off on my floor. The next morning, I checked out and moved into an Airbnb. Check the cameras and my phone logs. You'll see I've had no dealings with either of them and I'm tired of saying it." I angrily hit the table. "I wish they'd leave me alone."

"Calm down." She tells me.

"How am I supposed to calm down when I'm headed to jail for this lying, slick back, barracuda looking trick? You know, it's best I go to jail tonight. Tell them to come on. The way I'm feeling right now. Please take me to jail."

"Hush. Ava, hush."

"Jamia, I'm so sick of this. Every time things seem to turn in my direction, it feels like I'm t-boned and left spinning in circles."

"We're going to figure this out. I spoke to Levar and he's waiting to sign your bond. It may take a few hours, but we'll get it paid as soon as it posts and we're going to fight this."

"What's the point? Every day it's something. Maybe being in jail will give me a night of peace without the stress. I'm tired Jamia."

"Then let me do the fighting. Ava, people lie, data doesn't. In the meantime, she's been granted a temporary protection order which means you have to stay away from her."

"You mean like I've been doing, or should I change countries?"

"You're not going anywhere. Sign these." She hands me two pieces of paper. "This gives me authorization to contact your wireless and email carrier to pull your records."

"Can't I give you access to my online account?"

"Yes, but it won't give me the physical transcripts of your text messages to prove she's lying. Write down your username and password."

"When they do, I'm suing her ass for defamation. Wait, I changed my number a few weeks ago."

"You did, didn't you? Do you know the exact date?" she asks.

"Um, I believe it was the first of December."

Jamia smiles. "Got it."

The door opens and an officer comes in.

"Ma'am, I'm here to transport you."

"Do you have to put the cuffs back on? I promise not to run."

"Yes ma'am, it's protocol."

"Then let's do this."

"Ava, you'll be out soon." She tells me.

I walk out singing. "Nobody knows the trouble I've seen. Nobody knows but Jesus."

chapter twenty-four

One hundred and twenty-seven minutes of being transferred, booked, fingerprinted, a mug shot taken and read my formal charges, I'm sitting in the coldest holding area ever. Thank God I put on flats this morning instead of heels, pants, and a blazer. I'm hoping I don't have to see how I'd look in a jumpsuit. Finally able to use the phone, I call June.

"Hey, it's me. June, stop crying. I'm okay. Girl, she lied like I've been sending her texts and emails threatening her and her unborn child." I laugh at her mention of Katrina and the bald head baby. "Seriously, I wish they'd leave me alone and go on with their life. Yeah, Jamia is already working on it. No, don't you dare come down here. Levar is going to sign my bond. Hush. Hopefully, I'll be out of here soon. Love you too."

Hanging up, I sit in the corner closing my eyes.

"Okay Lord. I told you I trusted you and I do, but could you give your girl some grace? Geesh. All of this in one day God, really? Could you not have warned me to put on tennis shoes to wade through all this mess." Exhaling. "Yet, I will not be defeated because Lord, it's in your hands. Deal with my enemies and avenge my name.

And God, it wouldn't hurt if you did it expeditiously. Amen."

"Do you really believe in that stuff?" a young lady asks from across the room.

"Prayer?"

"No, God." She clarifies.

"I do."

"Why? What makes you believe in someone you can't see or touch?"

"The same reason I trust the air we breathe even though we can't see it. I believe it'll do what it's been designed for. God, same reason. He's never let me down, even when I thought He had. Hi, I'm Ava."

"Bailey. What are you in for?"

"Stalking and harassing the nutcase who's dating my ex."

"Ah, you couldn't let go, huh."

"Child I've let go, burned the bridge, cancelled all subscriptions and still can't get free of them. Trust me when I say, they aren't worth it."

"Then why are you in here?"

"It's easy for folk to accept your guilt then it is to investigate. Afterwards, they'll make you fight like hell to prove your innocence."

"Sounds to me, ole girl must think you're a threat to their relationship?"

"I can't see why. Dude couldn't get another chance with me if it meant the end of global warming."

"Dang. He must have really f'ed up."

"If trying to kill me falls into that category, yes. Anyway, why are you here?"

"Possession of Mary-Jane. This cop pulled up while I was sitting in my car and said he smelled weed. He wasn't lying. I was smoking like a freight train." She laughs. "I tried explaining my mom is at the end of her fight with cancer, I have a fifteen-year-old sister, school, two jobs and things have been rough. So I use weed to calm my nerves, but he wasn't having it. He arrested me and now, I have to pray mom doesn't die before I'm released."

"How long have you been waiting?"

"Since about three this morning. My sister is trying to get in touch with our flaky father to post my bail, but I won't hold my breath. Which means, I'll be here until the judge lets me out or he shows up."

"Wow. Bailey, I can't imagine how hard it must be to watch your mom suffer while carrying the weight of an adult on your shoulders. You look like a child yourself."

"I'm 22."

"Too young to have so many responsibilities. What's your last name?"

"Clark."

"Bailey Clark, call your sister and tell her, I'll pay your bail."

"Why would you do that when you don't even know how much it is or me?"

"Because I can, and I need something positive after all this foolishness." I admit. "Besides, you could use the break too."

She stands. "You sure?"

"Yep. Go on."

I watch as she rushes over to the phone. She comes back with tears streaming down her face.

"Hospice is giving my mom two, three days to live. That's it. What am I supposed to do without her?"

"Oh Bailey."

I open my arms and she sit beside me, sobbing.

"God, this baby needs you. She needs you for strength, guidance, wisdom, protection, and provision. She needs you. God, she's been angry with you for a while, but at this very hour, hear my plea and answer. Although she doesn't understand, show up for her and her family. I even ask you to look after her mom while she lays on her bed of affliction. Cancer is taking a lot from them, but Father I decree it shall not take you. Give Bailey understanding and answer her question of why, so she knows she isn't alone."

"Gentry, pretrial is ready for you." An officer yells.

"God, heal her heart and let her turn to you instead of grief and anger, especially when she doesn't understand. And Father, dismiss this case as she has enough to deal with. In the name of Jesus, I pray. Amen."

She doesn't immediately let me go.

"Bailey, I know it can be hard to trust a God who we think allows bad things to happen. I've been there and for a long time I turned my back on Him, yet He never turned His on me. Now, I know no matter what happens, good or bad, I trust God with my life."

"Why?" she sits up wiping her face and her voice clouded with anger. "Why is it easy to trust Him when you're in jail for something you didn't do? If He's so powerful, why didn't He stop it?"

"I didn't say it was easy. I trust God because He kept me when I was silly, simpleminded, foolish, and undeserving to live. Sure, there are things I wish I didn't have to go through. Being in jail for something I didn't do is one of them. However, I realize had God stopped me from being here, I never would have met you."

I stand. "See, there's a purpose to everything."

"Thank you, Ava."

"If some reason you're not here when I get back, call 901-274-0091 and talk to Jamia. She'll know what to do."

"274-0091, Jamia." She repeats.

chapter twenty-five

Thirty minutes later, I'm taking back to the holding area. I stop by the phone to call Jamia, explaining Bailey's plight and asking her to relay the information to Levar to take care of her bond.

"Still here." Bailey waves when I go over to take a seat.

"Not for long. We're going to get you home today."

"While we're waiting, do you mind telling me more about God?" she inquires.

"Of course not. However, I must warn you. I'm no Bible scholar. See, I thought God was supposed to move whenever I called, change my situation when I was desperate, give me what I'd demanded while in the middle of sin or stop every bad thing from happening in my life. When He didn't, I spent a lot of years in anger and without Him. Only to realize, God wasn't ignoring me, I didn't truly know Him for myself. It took me almost being destroyed to trust Him."

"I hear you Ms. Ava, but it's hard not to be mad when I know my mom is dying and He has the power to heal her."

"He is healing her, although it's not in the way you were expecting. Bailey, sometimes it isn't God who fails us, it's our expectations."

We continue to talk until Bailey falls asleep with her head on my leg. Me, I've been staring at the clock on the wall. Four long, cold, and hungry hours later, a jailer calls Bailey's name saying she's moving to an upper floor and will have to change clothes since no one has posted her bond."

"Can you check again?" I ask her. "My boyfriend should have taken care of it."

She leaves and Bailey looks over at me for assurance. Thirty minutes go by, and another officer calls the both of us.

"Y'all been processed out. Let's go."

"God's timing." I say to her.

We walk upfront to sign out and get our personal effects. Heading towards the door, I look over at Bailey. "You don't have a coat?"

"I wasn't wearing one when I got arrested, but I'm okay. I'll walk over to the gas station and see if they'll let me charge my phone to find a way home."

"No ma'am, I'm not leaving you here alone in this cold."

"You're already doing enough."

Before I can respond, I'm bear hugged by Levar as Jamia laughs.

"Are you okay? They didn't hurt you, did they?"

I grab his face, kissing him. "I'm good and no. It was only a few hours."

"Okay, you two." Jamia chuckles. "You must be Bailey?"

"Yes ma'am."

"It's nice to meet you. I'm Jamia and this is Levar. I was able to pull your documents to see you're charged with a misdemeanor drug offense for a small amount of marijuana. You'll have to appear in court tomorrow at 9 AM at which time I'll speak to the prosecutor about pleading this down to community service."

"Do I come back here?" she inquires.

"Here's my card. Let's meet at my office at 8." Jamia says.

"Um, ma'am. I don't have money to pay you but if you let me set up a payment plan—

"You let me worry about that." I stop her. "Let's get you home."

Getting into Levar's truck, I lay my head on the seat. He takes my hand and I look over at him.

"Ms. Ava, you mind if I ask a question?"

"Of course not."

"Why would the lady be threatened by you when you have a husband who you clearly love?"

Levar glances at me with a smile.

"We're not married."

"Not yet." He adds and I blush.

"Oh. You couldn't tell by the way y'all look at each other." She remarks settling into the seat.

"I like you." Levar says before asking for her address and putting it in the GPS.

A few minutes away, he looks at her through the rearview.

"Bailey, would you like to stop and get something to eat. I know it's been a long day."

"Can we? There's a McDonald's coming up on Lamar. I think I have enough for cheeseburgers."

"Order whatever you want, I got it." He tells her.

When she's done, she tries giving him the dollars and change she has. He refuses. Pulling in front of the house, I get out to help her carry the drinks. Levar follows.

"Bailey." A girl jumps up from the couch. "You're home."

"Ms. Ava and Mr. Levar, this is my sister Briley."

"It's nice to meet you."

An older lady comes down the hall and Bailey introduces her as Lorraine, her mom's night nurse.

"Ms. Lorraine, how is she?" Bailey questions.

"She's sleeping and," she pauses.

"Just tell me."

"Bailey, your mom's body is shutting down and most likely she will not wake up again. At best and from experience, she may have at least two days."

"Is she in pain?"

"No, we're keeping her comfortable. You can go in and talk to her. She can hear you even if she doesn't respond."

Bailey thanks me again and I let her know I'll pick her up in the morning. Briley takes her hand and they both go into the bedroom.

"I've only known this baby for less than eight hours and my heart aches for them. Do they have any family?" I ask her.

"A father who's in and out fighting the demon of addiction. Other than that, it's been the two of them. I've been their mom's night nurse for over a month and I've yet to see any other family or friends. Their mom, bless her heart, took precautions to make sure they'll be okay financially but emotionally, they're going to need help."

"Is it okay if I leave my number with you to call if there's anything we can do?"

"Of course."

chapter twenty-six

Getting inside the truck, I feel like screaming.

"Lord why is life so hard. They're only babies Levar and having to say goodbye to their mom. It's three days before Christmas. They should be wrapping gifts, decorating the tree, dressing in matching pajamas and watching Hallmark with hot chocolate. Instead—man." I exhale. "When you think your life is hard, you come into contact with someone having it worse. Here I am thinking I've got problems when they're nothing compared to what they are about to face."

"That's not true. Your problems are valid and aren't lessened by theirs. Y'all are simply going through something different at the same time. Nevertheless, we'll be there for them as much as they'll allow while taking care of you too."

I look back at the house.

"I hope I didn't offend you by inserting myself without you asking for my help."

"You didn't."

"You can be honest with me."

"Truth is, having you here scares the crap out of me. I'm not used to this and well, you. I've never had a man care for me without it costing me something and causing hurt. I guess what I'm asking for is a little patience and if I unintentionally shut you out, call me on it."

"Ava, I'm willing to do my part in this relationship and I'll be as patient as you need, under one condition."

"What's that?"

"Please don't get mad."

I sit up. "Just say it."

"Promise you won't use your need for patience as an excuse forever."

"Excuse? Is that what you think I've been doing all this time, making excuses?"

"No, I didn't mean it like that. Let me explain."

"I'll have you know I'm fighting every day to survive the hell I was given. Even when I didn't want too, I got up to face life that kept knocking me down. With very little strength, I got up. It hurt to breathe, I got up. Attacked in my own home. I got up. And you got the nerve to think my ask for patience is an excuse? Well, screw you Levar. Screw you and this jacked up world. Screw you." I scream.

He tries to grab me.

"No. Please take me to my truck? Please."

We drive in silence until we reach the parking lot. Not giving him a chance to say anything, I get out.

Making it to the driver's side door, I remember I don't have my purse or keys.

"Got da—

"Here." Levar says coming up handing me my bags. "Will you allow me to explain?"

"You think I'm making excuses. No further explanation needed."

"That's not what I said. Ava, wait." He says grabbing my hand. "Sometimes what we face isn't to destroy, it's to distract. When my sister was murdered, the grief distracted me from everything I'd been working towards. I couldn't focus and I took advantage of people's patience. It didn't matter how bad I treated them, I expected them to wait, accepting whatever I dished out since they knew what I'd gone through. Until one day, Michael served me a hard dose of reality.

He said, their patience wasn't for who I was, in the moment, but who they knew I could be beyond it. Yet, they wouldn't put up with my anger, lashing out and mood swings forever. I had to choose. Either stay angry or I could see what was on the other side of the pain. So, I went to counseling and found a better way to channel my energy instead of using it to push away those I love."

"Thanks for the cozy story, but it still sounds like I'm using patience as a crutch."

"Baby." He sighs. "Had I not gotten better, there'd be no Small Sticks and the best part, I never would have met you. Ava, I'm in no way rushing you to heal, but don't allow the circumstances to distract you from seeing your way out of darkness."

"And I'm guessing you're my compass?" I sarcastically ask.

"It's possible, but even if I'm not, don't miss who might be." He gives me a kiss on the cheek. "Let me know you've made it home safe."

He waits until I'm in the truck before walking away.

"Lord, what am I doing? Ugh." I scream hitting the steering wheel.

I sit there until I hear my phone ringing in my purse. Pulling it out, I see its June.

"Hey." I somberly answer. "I'm fine. June, I'm okay. Not yet. I'm sitting in my truck." I look in the rearview mirror. "He's sitting in his truck watching me." I let out a long exhale, pressing the start button and letting the phone connect. "What does he see in me?" I begin to cry. "With all the baggage I bring, what could he possibly want with me? Even after yelling at him, he kissed me on the forehead and said to text him when I make it home."

"Ava, why are you doing this to yourself? Girl, don't you know baggage can be unpacked or better yet, thrown away? This may be hard to hear, but you're the one who keeps looking through them hoping the contents will change then being mad when they don't. Sis, you deserve to be loved. The good, butterfly feeling, tingle in your toes, twinkle in your eye, memory making, back breaking, longsuffering, growing old, it doesn't hurt unless it comes with an orgasm kind of love. Yet, you'll never get it when you keep believing you don't. That man loves you, but you can't expect him to wait forever."

"He said the same thing." I exhale. "What if I can't love him back?"

"Why would you think this?"

"Andre once told me I never required him to put forth any effort into our relationship and he was right. Yet, I realize I didn't require it from him because it would mean I'd have to give it back. June, Levar is a great man, and I don't want to damage him."

"Then don't."

"It's easier said than done."

"No it isn't. It's getting up every day putting forth an effort to be greater than who you used to be. Ava, your bloodline was tainted by this curse of love equates to pain. In fact, it started from the moment you were conceived, and you can either change it or let it continually chain you. Whew, that's a word. Preach June."

"I hear you."

"Are you listening though?" she asks.

"Yes."

"Good. Now, tell me about your jail chronicles while you drive home."

chapter twenty-seven

An hour of pacing and talking to myself, a shower and glass of wine later, I get into bed. I text Levar to let him know I'd made it home and his only response was, get some sleep. Turning off the lights, plugging my phone to the charger and connecting it to the Bluetooth speaker, I shuffle the music.

"You rescued me. You rescued me Lord. I'm mighty grateful you rescued me." Plays through the speaker. *"I was low down dirty, but you cleaned me up."*

A sob erupts from the damaged parts of my soul.

"Lord, you rescued me, yet I keep finding my way back to the place of bondage."

"If God be for me what can stand before me?" the Psalmist sings.

"Father, while I believe help my unbelief. Help the parts of me struggling to see me healed. Help the parts of me which thinks I don't merit love. Help the parts of me still clinging to the broken shards of despair even after you've healed me. You rescued me when I didn't deserve it and I'm throwing it back in your face. Father, forgive me."

"It was amazing grace, how sweet the sound that saved a wretch like you and me. I once was lost, but now I'm found."

"Forgive me for consistently acting ungrateful. Forgive me, Father please. Please don't allow me to stay stuck when the chains have already been removed. Don't allow me to miss this chance. Let me see the way out. Let me see you. Amen."

The next morning, I'm up before the sun staring at the ceiling with the music still playing.

"Hello God. I feel you in the darkness of the night and in the valley, you're right by my side. And though I think it strange, each time I run from pain when that's the tool you use to make me right, so I say Holy, Holy, Holy, Holy."

I quickly sit up.

"God no longer am I yielding to this woe is me spirit. You've saved me, over and over again and I'm tired of misusing the time I have." I stand up, beginning to pace. "I'm alive, in my right mind, all my limbs work, got a roof over my head, food in the refrigerator, an appetite, money in the bank, a new house waiting, the ability to clear my name and a man who's willing to love my almost destroyed self. There will be no more excuses as to why I can't. You've given me chance after chance. Now, it's time I give me a chance and I'm ready. Thank you, Jesus and amen."

I walk around.

"A change is coming for me if I stand strong and believe. There's no reason to doubt, I know He's working it out. It's turning around for me. It won't always be like this. The Lord will perfect that concerning me. Sooner or later, turn in my favor." I sing. "It's turning around for me."

After getting dressed, I grab my things remembering I didn't get Bailey's address last night. Inside the truck, I text Levar. A few minutes later, he sends it back with well wishes for the arraignment.

Pulling up to Bailey's house, I get out and ring the doorbell. A gentleman opens the door.

"Hi, I'm Ava here to pick up Bailey."

"I'll be right out." I hear her yell from behind him.

Inside the truck, I fasten my seatbelt.

Bailey opens the door. "Good morning."

"Good morning sweetie. How's your mom?" I ask once she's inside.

"The same. I asked her not to hold on until I get back. Is that selfish?" she questions.

"No, it's being human." I assure her.

"I don't even know if she can hear me."

"Trust that she can."

"How are you so hopeful?" she questions.

I tell her a little about my childhood and things I had to deal with before I was her age. "I've found it's better to be hopeful than hopeless. Ful, F-U-L means full of versus less L-E-S-S that means without. As long as I stay hopeful there's opportunity for things to get better."

"Hopeful." She repeats.

We meet Jamia at her office before walking the block to the courthouse. Bailey's hearing is in courtroom three while I'm in one. I'm sitting in the back waiting when Katrina walks in wearing a Mommy-to-be shirt.

I shake my head.

She sits at the front with her arms folded and a smirk.

I wait through the five or six cases before me. Jamia comes in taking a seat next to me. She passes me a note and pen.

When did you change your phone number?

I think December 1

I pass it back.

"Calling case number 21RTN-70932, the State of Tennessee versus Ava Gentry."

"Your honor, Jamia Dubose for the defendant."

"Jacoby Wright for the state."

"Ms. Gentry, you're before this court for purposes of arraignment on count one, stalking, a class A misdemeanor punishable by up to a year in prison and count two, harassment also a class A misdemeanor punishable by up to a year in prison. Do you understand these charges?"

"Yes, your honor."

"How do you plead?"

"Not guilty."

"Ms. Gentry, I see here you were released on your own recognizance. While that may be the case, you shall have no contact with the victim in any way whether directly or indirectly. You are prohibited from threatening offenses, the use of alcohol, controlled substances and any kind of firearms or other weapons. If there are any violations, bond will be revoked. Do you understand these conditions set before you, Ms. Gentry?"

"Yes sir."

"Very well. We will set the preliminary hearing for the next available date, which is Monday, January tenth at 9 AM in this courtroom. Next case."

Jamia and I walk out to meet Bailey. I'm about to ask how things went with her when Katrina rushes up.

"You're going to jail. Do you hear me?" she screams.

"Ma'am, everybody can hear you. Please move along." Jamia instructs.

"No one is talking to you." She points.

"Ms. Gaskins, what are you doing?" Mr. Wright asks stepping in front of her. "You're not supposed to have any contact with her. Come on and I'll walk you out."

"She's the one harassing me. Make her leave. I have every right to stand right here."

"Can we go?" I ask Jamia.

"Yes. I'll be in touch."

"Wow, she's a few nickels short of a dollar." Bailey says causing me to laugh.

chapter twenty-eight

I'm sitting outside of the property which will soon be mine after meeting with a settlement agent to secure the earnest money. Following, I met with Lakita, the builder, inspector, and appraiser. Then it was a lady from their design center. I kept most of the finishes and colors from the previous buyers, only needing to make a few adjustments.

I wasn't expecting things to go so fast due to the holidays, but God is working things out for me. If all goes well, I'll be able to close the first of March.

"Any day Lord." I speak remembering the day I lost my job, going by Roundtree Estates and praying the exact thing. Tears fill my eyes as I look at the sign depicting my name.

Welcome to your New Home: Gentry Family

"God, you kept your promise. Now, I'll keep mine. No more woe is me."

Wiping my face, I start the truck and forty minutes later, I'm outside Levar's house. It's Christmas Eve and I don't know if he's home. Exhaling, I get out to ring the doorbell when the garage goes up.

"Ava? I was headed to your place to drop off your gift. One second."

He goes to his truck, returning with a bag.

"Thanks, but I came to apologize."

"You don't have too." He tells me.

"Let me say this. I apologize for the way I've taken your grace for granted. Even when you didn't know me, you calmed me during a panic attack. You showed up for me, willing to fight when I didn't have the strength to swing. Then, the parts of me you've come to know didn't run you off. Instead, you're willing to love me, and I keep pushing it away. In some ways, I've done the same to God. Falling into this woe is me valley, refusing the ladder which has been in reach all this time. I tell God I'm afraid of the darkness then recoil at the light He's sent through you, June and all my new family. You were right to ask me not to use patience as an excuse long term. I wasn't in the right mind frame to hear it."

"What's different now?"

"Me." I chuckle. "Between last night and this morning, I asked God for forgiveness and now, I'm asking you. Will you forgive me for taking advantage of your grace?"

"Ava, of course I forgive you."

"I've also come to terms with the fact, I can either let my past chain me or change me. I'm choosing the latter. Therefore, I don't need you to save me anymore."

"Okay."

"But I do need you to love me. If you'll give me another chance."

He walks up, cupping my chin. "Ava, I love you."

"But." I laugh moving his hand. "There's always a but. Go ahead."

"I may have forced myself into your life without giving you a chance to invite me in and I apologize. I thought I could be what you needed to get through all you're facing when the reality is, I can't. Yes, I can pull you out of the darkness, I can love the hell out of you, and I can make you happy outwardly but if you never change inwardly, you'll find the way back to despair. Ava, you need time with you to heal and figure out who you are. If not, you'll continually pull from broken pieces. Will you take time to deal with everything? Baby, look at me. Take the time Ava needs to properly heal and when you're ready, come get your man."

He pulls me into a hug, and I cry before he kisses me on the forehead.

"Merry Christmas Ava."

"Merry Christmas Levar."

Getting home, I open his gift. My mouth falls open at the pair of strappy Louboutin heeled sandals.

For our night of dancing. Merry Christmas Babe.

New Years' Eve, I'm sitting on the patio of the cabin I rented last week with a Chicks & Cigars Cherry infused cigar, glass of Cognac, and music. The fire pit is going, and I'm wrapped up holding a pen against the blank notebook, I begin to write.

Dear eight-year-old Ava,

Girl, we've been through some things in this here life of ours and while I wish time was better to us, it hasn't been. Yet, it's not our fault. It was never our fault. The things we had to witness, the abuse inflicted upon us, the blame we were made to take, and the darkness we were subjected too wasn't our fault. I don't care how much it was drilled into our mind. We weren't to blame. Yet, we're going to carry this burden for the next thirty years. Truth is, it's going to cause us a lot of pain and loss. The loss of our dignity, time, peace, health, finances, faith, joy, and sanity. We're going to spend thirteen years in a loveless relationship because no one ever made us feel worthy of it. We're going to suffer, a lot, by the hands of people but we're going to survive. Child, I can go on and on. Instead, we're absolving ourselves of this burden. Sure, I wish we could get back the time, but at this point, all we need is our life. With life comes hope.

So, here's what we're going to do.

1. We're not wasting anymore tears on what doesn't deserve it.
2. We're forgiving us.
3. We're going to continue to fight the enemy, lies, past and for our present and future.
4. We're going to release everything we've lost, grieve it, and heal.
5. We're going to embrace us while getting to know who we are.
6. We're going to accept what we can and faith what we can't.
7. We're going to love ourselves.
8. We're going to believe in our gifts, strength, and purpose.
9. We're going to live.
10. We're going to find a church home and build a personal relationship with God.
11. We're going to love and be loved.

12. *We're going to celebrate the small and big wins.*

13. *We're becoming a homeowner.*

14. *We're going to love on our beautiful niece.*

15. *We're going to forgive.*

16. *We're releasing everything that tried to hold us down.*

17. *We're going to send Katrina and Andre's ass to jail.*

18. *We're going to get our man!!!*

I shake out my hand to release the penned-up energy from writing long and fast.

Ava, we're going to be alright. We've already been through too much not to be. So, girl buckle up. It's going to be turbulent for a while. Nevertheless, we will survive. We have too. There's much more for us to experience.

"We've experienced enough of the bad. It's time to see what else there is." I say to the wind in hopes of God hearing.

chapter twenty-nine

When the music pauses, I look down to see June's picture on the phone's screen. Swiping to answer the Facetime, I see her face of tears. I quickly sit up.

"June, what's wrong? Is it the baby?"

"She kicked. The baby. I felt her kick." She tells me with more tears falling. "Oh my God. I've never felt this." She sobs.

"Oh sister." I pause letting her cry. "I'm kicking your tail. You scared me."

She laughs while wiping her face.

"I told her to wait." Grant hollers.

"Hush, snitcher." She throws a pillow at him. "He was crying too."

"Gul, let me see my baby. Calling me all dramatic."

She moves the phone down to her stomach.

"Hey sweet girl. Thank you for letting us know you're okay. Auntie loves you."

"How is auntie?" she asks.

"Eh. So, so. I'm enjoying the view." I turn the camera around.

"It's beautiful, and I pray it's giving you the time and peace you need to return healthier, happier and um, holy." She giggles. "I had to keep with the h's."

"You're a mess and I love you. Yes, the time alone is much needed. I'm not foolish enough to think I'll be completely healed in two weeks, but I'm sure going to try."

"Good for you. Happy New You sister and I pray this new year will bring you every good thing you deserve."

"Thank you. Happy New Year. I love you and Grant more than you know."

"We know and we love you too." Grant says coming into the camera. "Be safe up there."

At 11:57 PM, I have a bowl, incense and lighter as I prepare to burn the past. Lighting the incense, I begin to pray.

"Holy God of Heaven and Earth, I petition your throne tonight with a heart and mouth of repentance. As I say goodbye to the past and hello to the present, I need your presence. Father, as I release the sweet aroma of incense into the air, I pray you'll receive my prayer on the wings of this new day. Tonight, as we cross over into a new year, I enter in forgiving myself and those who have fault with me yet may never apologize. Tonight, as the old year passes away, so does the chains from my feet, wrist, mind, heart, and mouth." I pick up the paper lighting it. "As my past burns away, so does the limits I've placed on you and myself. God, thank you. Thank you for dealing with the stubbornness of me. Thank you for not getting tired of me. Thank you for speaking even when it seemed like I wasn't listening. Thank you for loving me through my current conditions."

I jump at the sound of fireworks going off.

"Well, it looks like I made it. Thank you for allowing me to make it into 2022. This year will be greater than the last because I'm different and claiming it to be so. I'm coming for everything you said I could have. While I do, God deal with my enemies, destroy the work of darkness and iniquities, avenge my name, and let me start anew. I denounce every word curse spoken over my life and I replace it with your word in Jeremiah 29 verse eleven. I come out of agreement with fear, generational curses, self-doubt, unworthiness, brokenness, and flesh. The past may have fooled me into believing I wasn't worthy, but it's a lie. I've always had value and even if it took me getting to this moment to realize it, I'm here now. I'm here, ready to take back my rights and my name."

I stand up and begin to walk around the patio.

"Shoot, I deserve happiness and I shall have it. I've got too much to live for to die now. I've overcome too much to constantly act like the enemy has the upper hand. Nawl, old funky devil. You had your chance and lost. So take your games, lies, workers and be gone. There's no more room here for you and your lease agreement is terminated.

Pack your bags, take your hands off my life, name, possessions, faith, and family, and go back to hell. You may have thought I was weak, but you let me get up and now I realize my strength. You thought I'd succumb to my injuries when God simply placed me in a coma to recover. Oh, but I'm here and I came to fight."

I jump around punching the air. "Ha, you may get a few licks in." I duck and dodge, pretending to be boxing. "That's alright. I got a coach in my corner, and He says all I got to do is stay in the ring because the fight is already fixed in my favor. You ready? I am because this fight is personal." I punch a few more times. "Winner by knock out, Ava Justine Gentry. And the crowd goes wild."

I stop and look up. "God, this fight is personal. I'm fighting for the marriage and the wedding which hasn't happened yet. I'm fighting for the children who haven't been placed in my womb yet. I'm fighting for my name. I'm fighting for relationships you've ordained. I'm fighting for the gifts I've yet to use. I'm fighting for the legacy of who I am. And God, I'm fighting for me. This thang is personal."

――――――――――

Two Weeks Later

"Good morning. We're here today, January 10, 2022, for the preliminary hearing of case 21RTN-70932, the State of Tennessee versus Ava Gentry. Upon a complaint filed on December 10, 2021, charging the defendant with misdemeanor offenses of stalking, and harassing. The defendant, Ava Gentry, is present and represented by counsel Jamia Dubose. The state is present and represented by Jacoby Wright, prosecuting attorney. Is the state ready to proceed?"

"Yes, your honor."

"Are there any sequestering of witnesses?"

"No your honor."

"Are there any other preliminary matters?"

Mr. Wright stands. "Yes, your honor. In light of new evidence, the state is moving for the charges against Ms. Gentry to be dismissed."

"Mr. Wright, what new evidence?" the judge asks.

"May I approach your honor?"

"You may."

I look over at Jamia who gives me a side eye.

"Your honor, the documents submitted to the courts have proven the text messages, emails and phone calls were not from the defendant. In fact, there's no evidence the defendant has contacted the complainant in months. On the contrary, our investigators have found the proof used to substantiate this claim of harassment and stalking were either falsified or completely made up causing undue stress on the defendant, along with time wasted on behalf of our office and this court's time. All of which will not be taken lightly. We apologize to the defendant for not doing our due diligence in the beginning."

"Mrs. Dubose, is there anything you'd like to add?"

"Yes, your honor. The complainant has been a constant thorn in my client's side. She had her arrested and charged based on bogus claims proven to be false. While I'm sure my client appreciates the apology from the prosecutor, what she desires is to be left alone."

"Ms. Gentry, on behalf of the state of Tennessee and this court, we apologize and the charges against you are hereby dismissed. You're free to go."

"Thank you, God." I exclaim.

Getting to the door, Katrina lunges at me.

"Ma'am, move along before your ass ends up in jail." The deputy tells her pushing open the door.

We wait until she's gone before walking out of the courthouse. Inside my truck, I turn on the phone and see a text from Bailey.

Bailey Clark: She's gone.

chapter thirty
Katrina

Getting to the car, someone forcibly grabs me.

"I thought you had this. You said she'd suffer. That doesn't look like suffering to me."

I look over to see Ava rushing to a truck.

"You had one freaking job." I'm pulled behind a van.

"Well, you were the one who messed up the evidence. How did you not think this through?" I snatch away. "You had to know they'd pull the phone records. Now, I'm the one who looks like a fool and the prosecutor is threatening to arrest me for filing a false report."

"I don't care. We had a deal. She goes to jail, and you get the man. Go back on yours and I'll do the same. Is that what you want?"

"No, but I'm tired. I'm tired of all of it. This isn't what I signed up for."

"Of course it is. You knew exactly what was going to happen the moment you agreed to the terms. So, stop whining and figure out the next move."

"Me, what are you going to do? I seem to be the only one getting my hands dirty while you call the shots. You had me pull my brother into this, and he could possibly

S

get fired and if I get arrested, I can lose my job. What are you sacrificing? Matter of fact, what's in this for you?"

"Let's just say, Ava is getting everything she deserves. I'll be in touch."

"Ugh." I scream.

Inside the car, my phone rings.

"Miguel, it's not a good time."

"I was fired today." His voice bellows through the Bluetooth. "I never should have agreed to help you."

"Dude, stop whining. You got ten thousand for your part in this. The part you didn't do well, by the way."

"I still lost my job."

"Then move, hell. You act like this is the only city with a police force." I scream.

"And you act like this won't follow me." He yells back.

"Get off my phone Miguel. I have bigger problems to deal with and they don't consist of my crybaby ass brother. Goodbye."

Getting home, I walk in throwing my purse.

"What's with you?" I jump from the sound of Andre's voice.

"Nothing."

"Does it have anything to do with the charges you put on Ava?"

"I don't know what you're talking about, and I don't feel good. I'm going to bed."

"Stop lying." His voice booms following me into the bedroom. "You've been lying this entire time. Tell me one thing, what's the end goal?"

"Andre please."

"What's the point of going after Ava?" he yells in my face. "Katrina, you better start talking."

"You." I yell back. "It's you. With her out the way maybe you'll choose me."

He pushes me down on the bed.

"Are you really this delusional?"

"Don't say that. I'm not delusional. I love you. Dre, I've loved you from the moment I saw you. You don't remember, but two years ago you came to my rescue. I'd had a break-in at my house, and you showed up. That night, you were the perfect gentleman staying until I could pack a bag then driving me to my brother's house. You even came to check on me a few days later. It was then I realized, we were destined to be. Only problem, the fat chick you were living with. I had to figure out a way to get rid of her. Murder wasn't an option though. Then I'd be in jail."

"Katrina." He yells. "Do you hear yourself? Lady, I was a police officer doing my freaking job. Hell, I've done the same thing with plenty robbery victims. You weren't special."

I roll my eyes. "Yes, I was. I saw the way you looked at me. Anyway, I was patient and planning how to get you for myself. I never had any intention on befriending Ava, but she showed up at the condos I was working one day, down about losing her job. The Godly thing was to pray for her. I did. Afterwards, I invited her to church, and she was nice. I planned to make her think you were cheating or something. What I didn't count on was you choking the snot out of her. Nonetheless, things worked out because we're here now."

"Hello, things haven't worked out sweetie."

"Then what are we going to do?" I sit on the side of the bed, crossing my legs.

"Trina, I'm going to jail. I don't know what your plans are."

"I'll wait for you." I quickly get up. "Once you're released, we can get married and move on with our life. Definitely relocating though because there's too many bad memories in this city."

"You have it all planned, but you never mentioned the baby. Are you even pregnant?" he inquires moving away from me.

"No. Well, not yet." I giggle. "An easy problem to fix. All we have to do is, you know." I form a circle with one hand, jabbing a finger through it. "See, easy."

"I can't have children."

"That's a lie. I overheard Ava telling somebody she was pregnant."

"If she is, it isn't by me."

"Then why were you at her hotel?" I place my hands on my hips.

"To talk to her, hoping she'll put in a good word with the DA to lessen my charges. The thing I've been trying to do since all this mess started. Wait. How did you know I was at her hotel?"

I look off.

"Are you following me?"

"That doesn't matter. Look baby, I'm sorry okay. I may have gone about things the wrong way, but I love you and if you give me a chance, I'll prove it. As for the baby thing, all we need is sperm. Yours may not work, but there's plenty of men whose do. Now, let's find a movie and cuddle."

"You're crazy and this isn't love. It's control and you need help."

"Oh, but when you do it, it's cool."

"What?"

"You wanted to control Ava and when you couldn't you, ah, ah, ah." I put my hands around my throat. "At least, I haven't killed you."

His eyes widen.

"Relax. I'm not going too. I love you."

"Then why continue to go after Ava?"

"Unfortunately, Ava's suffering isn't up to me."

"Who's it up too?"

"I can't tell you."

"You can't or won't."

"Can we drop this? I'm tired."

"I need some air."

"Where are you going? Andre, where are you going?"

When I hear the door slam, I throw the framed picture of us into the wall. Getting my phone, I dial a number. "We have a problem."

chapter thirty-one
Andre

I get into my car, burning rubber to get away from Katrina. I pull up at the hotel where Ava was staying.

"May I help you?" the guys ask.

"I need the room number for Ava Gentry. G-E-N-T-R-Y."

"We don't have a guest by that name."

"Check again." I bark.

"Sir, calm down. There is no Ava Gentry registered here."

I hit the counter before turning to leave.

Inside the car, I call Clay. He doesn't answer. I dial Langston's number.

"Hey. What's the officer's name who helped Ava? I'll explain later, but I really need his name. No, I'm not about to do anything illegal. Lang, please." He places me on hold. "Josiah Rainey, thanks. I'll call you back."

I press the contact number for the police department switchboard, and I'm finally transferred to his office.

"Lieutenant Rainey, this is Andre Powell. I need to talk to you about Ava. It's important."

An hour later, I reluctantly walk into the administrative offices of the police department. After waiting, I'm escorted to a conference room. Inside is Deputy Chief Uniform Patrol Samuel Oakley, another guy and Josiah.

"Look, I didn't come here to be interrogated. I believe Ava is in danger." I go on to tell them about the conversation with Katrina.

"Mr. Powell, do you know this officer?"

I pick up the picture slidden to me. "No. Why? What's this got to do with Ava?"

"His name is Officer Miguel Suarez. On Friday, December tenth, 2021, he attempted a traffic stop on Ms. Gentry. It was later determined he had no jurisdiction to do so. Do you know this lady?"

"Yeah, that's Katrina."

"What is your relation to her?"

"She's a friend."

"Isn't she expecting your baby?" Rainey asks.

"No. She lied and if y'all are trying to accuse me of something, save it. I had nothing to do with these games she's been playing."

"Then who is she talking about?" he asks referring to what I told him Katrina said about Ava's suffering.

"Do y'all honestly think I would have shown up here if I was guilty of helping her? Katrina is working with somebody, and Ava's life may be in danger."

"We know. Mr. Powell, in our investigation of Officer Suarez, we found out he's the brother of Ms. Gaskins. According to Suarez, he had plans to plant drugs in Ms. Gentry's car in an attempt to get her arrested."

I shake my head. "She has a brother. I didn't know and I begged Katrina to leave Ava alone. Her being arrested doesn't help me."

"No, but maybe she thinks getting Ava out the way is better. Which is why we need your help."

"Help how?"

Two days later, I show up at Katrina's house with roses and a bottle of wine.

"What's this?"

"An apology." I tell her. "I thought we could spend some time together before I accepted this plea from the prosecutor."

"Plea? What plea?"

"Fifteen years to be served at thirty-three percent with the remaining time on parole."

I see her trying to figure it out.

"It's almost five years."

"Five years." She screeches. "No. She can't do this to you."

"Who?"

"Ava." She screams.

"Katrina, come sit. I get you want to blame Ava, but this isn't her fault. I hurt her and now—

"No. No." She jumps up. "She could have talked to the prosecutor or dropped the charges. See, I knew I should have taken care of her." She paces back and forth.

"What do you mean? Did you plan to kill her?"

"Kill? No, I'm not a murderer. Just sent to jail. I want her to suffer too."

"What part aren't you getting." I scream.

"You don't have to yell."

"Obviously I do. I exhale. "You can be so frustrating. Babe, Ava didn't do this, I did. Please, you have to leave her alone."

"Five years. Dre, what am I supposed to do for five years? Why should she get to enjoy life while you're in a jail cell? She needs to suffer. Do you hear me? She needs to suffer and we're going to make sure of it."

"Who's we? Who are you working with? Is it your brother?" I question.

Her eyes widen. "How do you know about my brother? Doesn't matter." She waves her hand. "My brother is soft."

"Then who?"

"She'll find out soon enough. Now, what do you want to eat?"

She turns to walk into the kitchen.

"Why aren't you moving?"

"The police know." I open my jacket to reveal the wire. "They know about you and your brother's plan with the drugs."

"You were setting me up?"

"No, I'm trying to save you from going to jail for being stupid and if you keep this up, you'll be there a lot longer than me."

"But I love you." She tells me with tears streaming. "I love you so much. I'll do anything for you."

I go closer, stroking her face.

"Then tell me who you're working with?"

"I can't."

I push her away.

"What happens now?" she questions.

"You talk to the police." I reply, looking over my shoulder as the door opens.

chapter thirty-two
Ava

I'm led into a conference room at Police Headquarters.

"Good morning, Ms. Gentry. My name is Samuel Oakley, Deputy Chief of Uniform Patrol and this is Walt Riesling with Internal Affairs. You know Sgt. Rainey."

"Yes, good morning."

Please have a seat. We wanted to meet with the results of our investigation into the traffic stop conducted by Officer Miguel Suarez on Friday, December tenth, 2021. As of Monday, January tenth, Mr. Suarez is no longer an officer of the Memphis Police Department. He was stripped of all duties due to official misconduct. In lieu of jail time for his misconduct and the illegal drugs, Officer Suarez admitted to his role in the plot to have you arrested."

"Arrested?"

"Yes. Their plan was to plant illegal drugs in your car. However, because you resisted and asked for a supervisor, it foiled their attempt."

"Their, as in Katrina and Andre?"

"Fortunately, Mr. Powell was not involved." Oakley says. "We spoke to him yesterday after he contacted Lieutenant Rainey in fear for your life."

"Then who?"

Josiah hands me a picture of Katrina. "His sister."

"This bitch." I angrily state pushing the picture away. "My apologies for the language, but she's trying to make my life hell like I've done something to her."

"It's not what you've done. It's more like what you won't do." Riesling states.

"What do you mean?"

"According to Suarez, all of this was for you to drop the charges against Mr. Powell."

"I keep telling the dummy me getting arrested won't change the outcome of Andre's case. He's going to jail with or without me."

"You're right."

I jump at the sound of Andre's voice.

"Ava, I'm sorry."

"You're sorry?" I angrily rise causing the chair to roll back before rushing over to him beginning to hit and push.

"Ava, stop." I hear Josiah, feeling him pull me away.

"No. Let me beat his ass. I'm sick of him." I lunge. "This Negro has made Katrina think he's the victim, like

I'm at fault. I was arrested, had a gun pulled on me by her brother, lied on and God knows what else she's planning. All because he can't man up."

"She's right."

"I know I'm right, trick. Even after you attacked me, when I could have bashed you on social media, I've stayed quiet. You keep showing up and I haven't reported any of it to the police. Each time, I ask you to do one thing. One thing." I yell. "What is that Dre? Huh, what?"

"To be left alone." He somberly states.

"To be left the fuc—heck alone." I shove him. "Yet, you can't even do that. Well, I meant what I told you last time. I'm going to fight you and everybody else to be free. So, tell your baby mammy to let me be or she'll have the bald head baby in jail."

"She's not pregnant. She lied."

"Shocker." I turn to the others. "You said the officer isn't getting jail time, but what about Katrina."

They all look at each other.

"What aren't y'all telling me?"

"She's working with someone else."

"Who?" I ask crossing my arms.

"We don't know."

I chuckle. "Wow. She keeps getting away with causing hell in other people's lives."

"I promise she's done." Andre says. "We just have to figure out who else—

"There is nobody else. Katrina is playing y'all and now I'm supposed to take your word that she's done. I'll say this. Katrina and her brother may not do jail time, but I'm going to make sure everybody knows who y'all are. I'm done being nice."

"Ma'am, please do not take matters into your own hands. We're confident Ms. Gaskins won't be bothering you anymore." Oakley tries to assure me.

"Chief Oakley, it's sweet you believe Katrina. I don't. However, I have no plans to do anything to her. Now, if this meeting is over."

"Here's a copy of the final investigation. If you have any more problems or questions, don't hesitate to contact me. We apologize for not being able to do more." Riesling says.

"Story of my life." I reply grabbing the paper and my purse.

Josiah walks me to the door. "If Katrina is working with someone else, we will find them. You know we have your back, right?"

"I do." I sigh. "Josiah, you and Naomi have been a blessing to me in more ways than you know. I only wish we could have met under different circumstances instead of getting entangled with me and my drama."

"I'm a cop. Drama comes with my profession." He laughs. "Seriously Ava. You're a part of our family now. We pray when this is over, you'll finally be able to enjoy the life God has always meant for you."

Amen." I hug him. "Thank you for always being willing to help."

"Any time. Oh, wait. I have something for you." He gets a folder from the desk. "My friend asked me to pass this along.

I give Andre one last glare before leaving.

Inside the truck, I open the folder to see the background check on Levar with a sticky note. *On paper he's a great catch.*

"Wow." I mouth flipping through to see the extensive file. She played no games when digging. He has good credit and no criminal record other than a few traffic tickets. There's also an article on his sister's death and a local writeup about Small Sticks along with his educational and employment history.

"Okay, Mr. Wilson."

chapter thirty-three

Later, I'm sitting in the middle of the bed staring at the words within the Facebook status box. *What's on your mind?*

Taking a deep breath, I tap the screen.

I must warn, this will be a LONG post as I've contemplated whether to share this with the world via this app.

<exhale>

For almost a year, my life has been in what feels like a whirlwind. On February 28, 2021, I ended a thirteen-year entanglement with Andre Powell. Truth is, I finally stood up for myself and he threw me out, destroying all of my belongings and almost destroying me. But I picked myself up, moved on and begin to rebuild my life. It was the hardest restart ever. Days and nights of crying and debating with a God I didn't have a relationship with. The moments when mistakes and regrets were speaking louder than my present kept me chained to a past I almost didn't survive.

Yet, in the middle of the storm, God would send a group of people to shine some light into the darkness I'd made my home. (June, Grant, Levar, Michael, Larissa, Josiah, and Naomi. I love them, by the way.)

I moved into a new place to stay, joined a new church, started seeing a new therapist, and got a new job. NEW ... Life was looking bright. Although there were specks of darkness still lingering, I was grasping for the new because it had to be better. Then, September 26, 2021, happened. The day Andre violently attacked me in my home. (He was arrested, and the case is ongoing.)

Nevertheless, I began to rebuild, AGAIN, only to find out one of the people who helped to rekindle my love for God was also sleeping with my now ex. Katrina Gaskins. Y'all, if this isn't bad enough, the trick has been making my life hell. From false charges of harassment, trying to plant drugs in my truck and lying about being pregnant. Yeah, it's been rough.

Here's my truth ... I almost succumbed to it. Until my sister, June, spoke into my life. She said, "Ava, your bloodline was tainted by this curse of love equates to pain. Either I can change it or let it continually chain me." That thang blessed me. LOL. So tonight, I'm declaring no more. If I continue allowing people and things to control the narrative of my life then who am I?

Baby, I've spent too many years being identified by the abuse, past mistakes and challenges this world has provided. As of today, Thursday, January 13, 2022, if you can't call me by my name, don't call me at all. If you got the wrong motives, move on. If you think I won't fight to survive, try me. This fight, it's personal because I'm fighting for me.

Ava Justine Gentry, a 38-year-old thick educated, smart, beautiful, black chick with curves and confidence. It may have taken time to find me, but I'm here now and I'm worthy of love, respect, trust, peace, and happiness. And I plan to get it.

Hi, I'm Ava and it's nice to meet you. 🫶 🤍

I press post dropping the phone on the bed as my heartrate picks up.

"I can't believe I did it."

A few minutes later, the phone vibrates.

June – Tru's Mommy: <a gif of Martin Luther King, Jr.>

I click on it and laugh.

Let freedom ring, let freedom ring!

June – Tru's Mommy: I'm so proud of you. Your post was everything!

Me: I can't believe I posted it. My heart is still beating fast.

June – Tru's Mommy: Opening yourself up to the public is always hard and there will be haters. However, trust YOUR process of healing. Whatever it looks like.

Me: I am. I can no longer allow other to quiet me. The only way I can live, I have to do it my (and God's) way. It starts now. I love you.

June – Tru's Mommy: I love you more. Go to bed. You've done what you can. Let God do what you can't.

Me: Yes ma'am. I'll call you tomorrow.

I fall back on the bed, letting out a breath.

chapter thirty-four

Sunday morning, I walk into a small church not far from the Airbnb. It's called Gracewood Baptist Church.

"Good morning. Welcome to Gracewood Baptist Church." The usher says. "This is your first time joining us, isn't it?"

"Yes ma'am."

"Well, come on in. There aren't a lot of us, but we love the Lord and serve Him faithfully. My name is Ruthie Feldman, the usher, secretary and first lady. My husband, Tobias is also the organist."

"Hi, I'm Ava."

"Ava, feel free to sit anywhere you like. Devotion is about to begin."

She hands me a program.

"You don't happen to sing, do you?"

"Yes ma'am, I sing a little." I admit and her eyes light up.

"Do you know *God is keeping me*?" she asks.

"Um, by Mississippi Mass?"

"Hold on." She rushes to the front, coming back with a piece of paper.

I look over the lyrics. "Yes ma'am, I think I can follow this."

"She can do it." She hollers out. "I'm sorry for putting you on the spot. The young lady who was supposed to sing came down with food poisoning last night and the choir has been looking forward to singing it."

"No problem." I lie quickly finding a seat and putting in my Air Pod to open YouTube. A few minutes later, Pastor Tobias begins playing the organ. When he belts out a Dr. Watts, my spirit leaps.

"We done bowed again, calling on your name. It's the Lord's blessing that we now enjoy." The deacon begins to pray.

By the time devotion is over, I'm tore up., Ten minutes later, I'm standing at the front of this church I've never been in, nervously holding the microphone as their four choir members are behind me.

"I want you to know that. Want you to know that. He blessed me and He kept me from all harm." I sing.

When the song is done, it feels as though a weight has been lifted.

"The Lord is surely in the blessing business church. Anybody believe it?"

"Yes sir." The members reply.

"We're so grateful for Sister Ava for joining us this morning and being willing to sing with the choir. Young lady, you have a beautiful gift and there's no amount of darkness that can shield what God has given you. Stay faithful."

I nod.

He gives his text, Jeremiah eighteen, verses one through four and begins to preach from his subject, 'A Reusable Mess." I attentively listen because it describes me.

"Jeremiah watches the potter work with this lump of clay, smoothing and shaping it. As he works it, Bible says, it doesn't turn out the way the potter desires. Instead of him throwing the clay out, he simply takes it off the wheel, rolls it into a lump and starts again. Verse six, God gives a message to Jeremiah. "*O Israel, can I not do to you as this potter has done to his clay? As the clay is in the potter's hand, so are you in my hand."*

In other words, we're clay being molded everyday by God. It matters not how many times he has to start over, as long as we remain moldable, there's a chance for us. Will it get hard? Sure. The process of forming clay isn't easy. It takes pressure, pulling and pressing. Sometimes, it'll take starting over one or ten times. Finally, after you've been formed, you'll have to sit a while to be hardened. It's during this period, the enemy will make you think you can't be used. But beloved, don't rush the process. You want to know why the hardening process is something you shouldn't skip? I'll tell you. Skipping the drying can compromise the end result.

What do you mean Pastor? If you place the pottery into the oven before it dries, it'll become frail, cracked, or will break once in the heat. Let me say it like this. If you don't go through the drying process, you may break when you have to go through the fire. Who am I talking to in this place? You've been through hell in your life, you don't feel worthy, got scars, been let down by folk, still sinning, fallen a few times and you might even be in a place of back sliding right now but there's hope. Hope to know, you are a reusable mess as long as you're in the hands of God."

After service, I go over to meet Pastor Tobias.

"Young lady, I pray you've enjoyed the service today."

"Yes sir. I didn't realize how much I've missed being in church. Thank you and Lady Ruthie for the warm welcome."

"Will we see you again?" she asks walking up.

"Definitely."

I drop my tithes in the offering box and head out.

"Lord, this feels like home. If it is, don't let me miss it. Amen."

chapter thirty-five

Two weeks later, June and I are standing at the graveside of Brenda Clark, Bailey, and Briley's mom. I look over locking eyes with Levar. I smile and he nods.

"We stand here today, in the midst of grief and pain to say goodnight to our loved one. There are no right words to take away what you are feeling, losing momma is hard. However, we must take joy in God's word of a promised resurrection. For Paul says in Philippians 3:20-21, *"For our citizenship is in heaven, from which we also eagerly wait for the Savior, the Lord Jesus Christ, who will transform our lowly body that it may be conformed to His glorious body."* This is why, even with tear-stained faces, broken hearts, and pangs of grief, we thank God for this day of celebration.

We can call it a celebration because Brenda knew God and in her knowing, her dying means her soul is now at rest from pain, sickness, and the cruelness of this mean world. We also recognize the body lying before us is not her but rather the earthly house in which she did not own, anticipating the day when spirit and body shall be united again at the coming of the Lord. It's then she'll move into the house with her name on the deed. While we'll miss her, we will allow memories, the abiding presence of God's Spirit and the fact we know where she is to strengthen, sustain, and comfort us.

To you, O Lord, we commend the soul of your dearly beloved servant, Brenda Clark. Forgive whatever sins she may have committed, on earth and welcome her into your everlasting peace. For we count it all joy to know that it has pleased you, our Heavenly Father, to take unto Himself our mother, wife, and friend. We therefore commit her body to the ground, earth to earth, ashes to ashes, dust to dust, looking for the blessed hope and the glorious appearing of the great God in our Savior Jesus Christ. Amen."

After the service, I take Bailey and Briley to their house where the small repast is being held. June and I had food catered to take the worry from them. An hour in, Bailey is chatting with a few of their church members, in the back yard, when a man rushes through the gate.

"Where is she?" he's screaming. "Where is my wife?"

He gets in Bailey's face causing me to rush over to her.

"Bailey."

"It's okay Ms. Ava. This is Patrick, my father."

"Bailey, where's Brenda? Where is she?"

"In New Park Cemetery." She flatly answers.

He falls onto his knees hollering out. "No, not my Brenda. Oh God."

She steps back folding her arms. "Can you hurry up? It's been a long day, months actually and your drama is exhausting."

He wipes his face with the back of his hand, getting up. Tears gone in an instant. "Don't you smart off at me little girl. I'm still the father."

"Yeah, not my choice. What do you want?"

"What's rightfully mine." He barks. "This house, half the insurance and a death certificate for social security."

"Dude, you must have hit a bad batch of drugs." Bailey counters. "Momma didn't owe you nothing. Y'all weren't legally married, and you bailed as soon as you found out she was sick. You were more committed to the glass pipe than any of us. Do Briley and I the favor of keeping it that way."

"This is my damn house and I'm not going anywhere."

"Correction, Pops. This is my house. Momma signed the deed over to me before she died. Now, the only things you're welcome to is the chicken in the kitchen, and your garbage bags in the garage."

She turns, walking away.

"Are you okay?" I ask her.

"Yes. This isn't new. Every few weeks he'd show up, begging momma to let him in. She would and two days later, he'd be gone along with the TV and money from her purse. When she got really sick, his visits lessened because she wasn't able to give him what he needed. Today is the first time we've seen him in months."

"I'm sorry."

"Don't be. I'm used to it." She tells me.

"Part of the problem. You should never get used to disappointment. Please don't ask me how I know. Instead, forgive people and stop giving them access to do it again."

"He's my father." She sadly says, looking at him.

"Which makes it even harder. However, sharing the same DNA doesn't give him the right to continually hurt you and staying loyal out of guilt destroys you, not them."

"I'm learning this. I keep thinking he'll change wanting to be here for his daughters, yet he never does. Now, I have a responsibility to protect Briley at all costs."

I hug her.

"Thank you, Ms. Ava for everything. I don't know how we would have made it without you and Ms. June."

"We're here for you."

"Will you stay a little while longer?"

"As long as you need."

She goes over to Briley and I begin to clean up the back yard. Turning, I bump into Levar.

"Hey. My apologies. I thought you'd left."

"No, I was out front talking to the pastor when I saw old dude bust through the gate. I came to check on y'all, but Bailey had everything under control."

"Yeah. She's a strong one for sure."

"So are you. How have you been?" he inquires.

"I've been good. How about you? Haven't seen much of you around the office."

"Great, tired from the traveling, preparing for the opening next month but it's worth it and easier with a trustworthy and hardworking staff." He bumps my arm.

"Well, you know I try." I joke.

"Has there been any issues with Felicia?"

"No, thank God. We were able to talk, she apologized, and I accepted. I didn't want to have friction between us, especially if we're going to work together."

"I agree which is another reason I wanted to talk to you."

"About?"

"This isn't the ideal place, but are things okay between us after the conversation on Christmas Eve? I don't want the "but" to make you think my feelings for you have changed. God led me to you, and I trust Him even when there's a delay to His plan."

"Levar, things are fine between us. Truth is, your "but" helped me to see I needed to unpack the baggage of the past I've been dragging all these years. I realize not dealing with them could potentially ruin my chance of a healthy, happy relationship while destroying the man God has sent to authentically love me. I won't say I've been completely healed in four weeks, but the process has started and it's stretching me pass my comfort and complacency. So, thank you for being bold enough to be honest with me."

"I don't know whether to say, you're welcome or kick myself if you're ending things for good."

I walk closer to him. "Say, you're welcome, Ava."

He grabs my face. "You're welcome, Ava."

"Ms. Ava." Bailey calls out.

"Can we finish this later? There's a lot we need to discuss."

"Of course." He kisses my forehead taking the garbage bag from my hand. "I'll take care of this."

chapter thirty-six

Standing in front of the floor length mirror gazing at myself. The off-shoulder grey sequin dress with the thigh split I ordered from Shein fit perfectly. It paired well with my strappy heeled sandals, silk press and soft makeup beat I was able to get.

You're still fat.

Those words spoken by Andre would have made me cringe because I used to hate this body. Who am I kidding? I hated the person too. Now though, they no longer faze me.

"Yeah, I'm fat Negro, but add in, she's beautiful, confident, educated, wealthy and free of you. Boom."

My phone vibrates with a notification of my car arriving. I grab my clutch, turn out the light and head for a night of fun.

Making it to the opening gala for Small Sticks, I'm met at the door by Grant.

"Ava, you look amazing." He tells me, kissing my cheek.

"Thank you. You're looking good yourself. Where's June."

"Gah-lee lil momma." June sings before he can answer. "Baby, you wearing that thang. And the face beat with the long hair don't care. Yeah, you bout to get your man sis."

"Hush and come on." I laugh taking her arm.

Inside the event space, we find our table and as Grant goes to get drinks, I go over to Larissa.

"Ava, ma'am you look absolutely amazing." She says then hugs me.

"You as well."

"Michael and Levar are preparing to give their opening speeches but let me introduce you to our families."

My stomach begins to do nervous flips.

"Relax." She takes my arm. "They're harmless. For the most part."

I stop.

"Kidding." She laughs. "Ava, this is our daughter Michaiah, son Lewis and Michael's parents, Randy and Vickie Stanton. This is my mom, Lisa Waters."

"Hi." They wave.

"These are Levar's parents, Levar, Sr. and Nellie Wilson and his sister Levitra."

"It's nice to see you again Ava." Levitra replies.

"You're more beautiful than Levar described." His mom Nellie remarks giving me a hug.

"You as well Mrs. Wilson."

"Please call me Nellie."

"Thank you. It's nice to finally meet all of you."

"My son tells me you can throw down in the kitchen and as you can tell, I love to eat." Levar Sr. laughs. "We're all anxiously waiting to taste that Kool-Aid he can't stop talking about."

I blush. "Yes sir. I'll have to fix you all some."

A few minutes later, Levar walks up to the microphone, and we take our seats.

"Good evening, ladies and gentlemen. My name is Levar Wilson and standing to my left is Michael Stanton. We are proud to be founders and operators of Small Sticks, Incorporated."

The crowd cheers.

"Tonight, we've come together with our families, friends, city dignitaries, media and business associates to celebrate this momentous occasion. This moment has been years in the making and while it hasn't been easy, it has been worth it. When Michael's daughter Michaiah and my sister Levitra were diagnosed with diabetes, we witnessed their struggle to do the very thing needed to survive. In their fight to live, we prayed for knowledge, wisdom, and instruction on how to help them and God provided.

This is why, we first acknowledge and are forever indebted to Him. We could not have done this without the blessings, plans and mercy of a God who gifted two black boys from South Memphis with the necessary knowledge, tools, and people to cultivate what you're witnessing. Secondly, Abraham and Tiffany Young. Vibrant souls God would use through friendship and finances. Their generosity helped to make this journey easier and we're grateful.

Lastly, but never least our families. Michael's wife Larissa who has had to put up with all our failures and successes, late night cram sessions, grumbling, complaining, and everything else. Sis, thank you. Michaiah and Levitra, the two we started this for."

He goes on to name their parents then the other heads of departments.

"As well as our head of Project Management and my partner, Ava Gentry."

My mouth falls open.

"Close your mouth sis, but I do believe that man just confirmed you as his." June whispers.

I excuse myself from the table, assuring June I'm fine.

After his speech, Michael gives information on the company with a demo of the devices and Buddi. When they're done, Levar is talking to a group of people when the song I asked the band to sing begins.

Forever Mine by the O'Jays.

"Forever mine. All because you're my kind. Aw, baby, I got what you want, you got what I want." The lead singer croons.

"May I have this dance?" I ask him.

"I apologize if what I said made you uncomfortable." He whispers in my ear.

I pull away to look at him before joining in to sing the lyrics. "I got what you want, you got what I want, and we were made for each other."

He smiles, closing the space between us. The song changes to *Love T.K.O.* by Teddy Pendergrass.

Three hours later, Levar and I pull up to the Airbnb. We talked on the way home, me filling him in on all that has happened since we last spoke.

I unfasten my seatbelt and start to open the door.

"Ava, thank you for tonight."

"I love you." I blurt. "I was going to surprise you with a decked-out room, music and dinner on Monday, Valentine's Day, but thought it would be too cheesy. Then you called me your partner in a room filled with everything I was imagining in my head, and I knew tonight was it." I chuckle. "Levar, I don't know if I'm even good at loving you. Until recently, I didn't love myself. Yet, you were willing to push through the darkness to show me there's light. You literally handed me your heart without knowing if I had the capabilities not to harm it. You've talked me through panic attacks, stayed when I lashed out and showed up when I was closed off. You waited for me when I didn't deserve it. Levar Tyrell Wilson, I want my man back."

He looks at me before grabbing his phone from the console.

"Do you have your identification?"

"Yes, why?" He doesn't answer while typing on his phone. "What are you doing?"

"Seeing if there are some redeye flights to Vegas."

"Vegas?"

"Baby, I'm too old to act like I don't know what I want. I want you and I have no plans to let you go again."

"Wait. We haven't talked or made plans. I'm sure you'll want a prenup and I'm about to buy a house. I just met your parents tonight. Levar." I exhale. "What will they think?"

He presses something on his phone and ringing fills the truck.

"Hey baby." His mom answers.

"Hey Ma, is Dad with you?"

"Yes, he's laying right here. Is something wrong?"

"No ma'am. I wanted y'all to know I plan on taking Ava to Vegas to get married. Tonight."

"No." She yells. "Sorry baby, your daddy got me watching some silly movie. Levar, you're grown and smart. I have no doubt you've made this decision with your heart and the way Ava looks at you, I can tell she loves you too. Let her know we've all been rooting for her."

"She heard you."

"Good. Send pictures and we'll see y'all when you get back."

"Thanks Ma."

He hits another button and the phone rings again.

"Hey brother." June answers.

"Sis, Ava and I are headed to Vegas to get married."

"Levar don't play with me. Are you serious? Are you serious?" she squeals.

"What, what's wrong?" we hear Grant asking.

"Levar and Ava are getting married."

"Aw hell, I thought you were in labor. Nobody is shocked by this." He says into the phone.

"Right, well maybe Ava." June laughs.

"I can hear you." I tell her.

"Girl, get out of your head. If marrying the fine man sitting across from you is what you want, hitch yo man sis. Love you. Bye."

"Shall I call Michael and Larissa too?"

"I only want to ensure, you're sure." I tell him. "Making big decisions while emotional will have you regretting them in the morning."

He unfastens his seatbelt, leans across the console, and opens the glove compartment pulling out a Tiffany box. Opening it, my hand flies to my mouth.

"I trust you and whatever business stuff needed can be handled when we return. Yes, it may seem impulsive, and I pray you won't regret this tomorrow. However, I know what I want and have since walking into that restaurant almost a year ago. I meant it when I said I prayed for you. After I healed from the grief of my sister, I vowed my heart to God until He sent me who He'd ordained for my life."

"How did you know it was me?"

"I didn't, my heart did. Babe, I'm not rushing you into anything. You can always tell me to wait, and I will. It was only a thought, seeing we're already dressed, and have next week off. Nevertheless, I will ask the question, leaving the decision up to you. Ava Justine Gentry, will you marry me?"

I keep staring at the ring on my finger with the biggest smile.

February 19, 2022, I became Mrs. Levar Wilson.

"Are you okay?" Levar asks removing his shades as we're laying by the resort's pool. "Having second thoughts?"

"Can I be honest?"

"Always." He sits up.

"After last night, I'm kicking myself for not marrying you sooner."

chapter thirty-seven

It's been three weeks since I married Levar and things have moved swiftly. We collectively met with our attorneys and created a prenup to protect the both of us after revealing my financial status. I also changed my last name on all important documents and moved into his home. We've decided to add his name to the house I'm purchasing since its brand new. On the conditions, he could claim one room for a man cave and add an outdoor kitchen to the back yard.

I wouldn't dare say no.

Earlier today, I finally cashed in on my birthday gifts. After a makeover, Levar and I had couple photos taken by Naomi. I'm excited to see the end results.

Small Sticks has taken off, blowing the first quarter expectations out the water. We're now in talks of manufacturing a device to deliver insulin by the end of the year.

Tonight, Levar and I are hosting dinner at our home. Even though we hired a private chef, I promised his dad, I'd make Kool-Aid and butter roll. Coming out of the bedroom, I get a call from Jamia.

"Hey Jamia, how are you?"

"Am I speaking to Mrs. Levar Wilson?" she chuckles.

"The one and only."

"Period. Look, I'm not going to hold you up, but I wanted to make you aware of the news I just received."

"Oh Lord."

"It's not bad. Andre's trial is set to begin Monday, March 28 at 9 AM. He can still accept the last plea up until then though which is fifteen years, physically serving five."

"If he accepts the deal, things will be over?"

"Yes."

"Then I'm going to pray he does."

"You and me both. I'll be in touch because you'll need to meet with the prosecuting attorneys in preparation to testify."

"Thanks Jamia."

"No problem. Have a great weekend."

"Everything okay?" Levar inquires wrapping his arms around me from behind.

"Andre's trial date has been set. March 28th."

"Great. You can finally close that part of your past."

"Thank God."

"Now, let's go and enjoy our family."

"Amen." I reply turning to kiss him.

Thirty minutes later, we're sitting around the table consisting of Levar's parents, Levitra, Michael, Larissa, June, Grant, Josiah, and Naomi laughing at a joke Levar, Sr., told.

"So, Ava will you be giving us grandchildren?" Nellie questions causing me to choke on my wine. She inserts a piece of salmon while waiting for an answer. "You do want children?"

"Mom, this is a topic for later." Levar says.

"It's okay." I tell him. "Honestly, Mrs. Nellie—Mom," I correct when she shoots me a look. "Honestly, I've never thought about it because I didn't think I was worthy of getting married. Growing up without seeing the joy of marriage, experiencing abuse, neglect, loss and etc., a family wasn't on my radar. I didn't love me, and I was in no position to love somebody else."

"What changed?" she asks.

"Me." I admit. "I could either rob myself of this." I wave my hand around. "Or get help to see beyond the darkness of my past. Man, I said I wouldn't cry tonight." I dab my face. "Most think it's every little girl's dream to find her prince charming, get married and have 3.5 kids, house and dog. For me, I was trying to survive. Yes, there were specks of happily ever after, but reality kept dealing me hands I believed happiness would never dwell in.

Even after meeting June and Grant, seeing their love gave me hope until I'd go home. I'm sorry."

"Please don't apologize for your truth." Larissa states.

"Ava, you have survived." Nellie says.

"Not yet, but I am surviving. It's an everyday struggle." I confess. "Nevertheless, I refuse to allow anything or anyone to overshadow the light each of you bring to my life. Yes, I can see children in our future. For the present, I want to enjoy my husband and family."

"To enjoying your husband, sis." June raises her glass of Kool-Aid.

"And to happiness, joy, peace and light." Levar adds.

Later the same night, Levar is in bed while I wrap my hair.

"Babe." He calls out. "Babe, you need to see this."

We meet at the bathroom door, and he turns his iPad to me.

I exhale. "I knew it was a matter of time."

"What do you want to do?"

"I'm going to report the page, text Jamia then enjoy my husband."

Grabbing my phone, I shoot a text to Jamia letting her know someone has created a fake Facebook page with my name and pictures. Somebody as in Katrina.

chapter thirty-eight

Two weeks later, I'm standing in the lobby of the DA's office when the Assistant District Attorney Marvin Willis comes up to me and Levar.

"Ms. Gentry, how are you feeling this morning?"

"It's Mrs. Wilson now." I say introducing Levar. "I'm ready to get this over with."

"Congratulations and it's understandable. Please follow me. May I get either of you some coffee, tea or water?"

"No thanks. Do you know if my attorney is here?"

"She is." He replies pushing open the door of the conference room allowing us to go ahead of him.

Jamia waves us over.

"Something is going on." she whispers. "I believe they've struck a deal."

"That's a good thing, right?"

"Depends on the plea."

Carl Houston, District Attorney enters. "Good morning, ladies and gentlemen. Thank you for coming this morning. I know we were initially scheduled to go over Ms. Gentry's testimony for Monday, however there's been a change. Late last night, our office met with the attorney of the defendant and was able to negotiate a final deal. In exchange for a guilty plea of the assault and rape, Mr. Powell has agreed to a total of ten years. Five for the assault and five for the rape to be served at thirty-three percent with the remaining time on parole."

"Will he have to admit what he did to me and why?"

"In pleading guilty, he will be asked to state what he's guilty of, however it doesn't mean he'll reveal the why."

"Is she allowed to give a victim's impact statement?" Jamia asks.

"Yes."

I look at Jamia.

"Are you okay with this?" she inquires.

"Will he be able to appeal?"

"No."

"With this plea, will he have to do the full thirty-three percent, and will the no contact conditions previously set, stand?" I question.

"Yes, he'll have to serve the full 3.3 years and we can assure the no contact conditions are pressed upon Mr. Powell, however, there is no lifelong order of protection. When the current order expires and he doesn't give cause as to why it should be extended, it'll end. Nonetheless, if at any time you feel threatened or in danger by him or anyone, don't hesitate to call the police. It's far better to have a trail of paperwork than to remain quiet and afraid." Mr. Willis answers.

I turn to Levar. "What do you think?"

"The sentence is quite lenient, but I'm on board with whatever feels right to you."

I close my eyes for a minute. "Yes, I'm good with it."

"How soon are you planning to go before the judge?" Jamia questions.

"We're keeping the date for Monday, hopeful to get this resolved. We'll meet at the courthouse at 9 AM." He tells us. "Ava, since this is only a sentencing hearing, you will be allowed in the courtroom. Do either of you have any more questions?"

We shake our heads no.

"I'll see you on Monday."

―――――――――――

Judge Linnell Coffee
Monday, March 28, 2022

"All rise. Twelfth District Court is now in session, the honorable Judge Linnell Coffee presiding. Please be seated." The clerk states. "This court calls the case of

People of the State of Tennessee verses Andre Donte Powell, case number 21T20092."

"Good morning. The court has been informed a deal has been reached in this matter. Is that correct?" I inquire.

"Yes Judge."

"Mr. Abernathy, have you made your client aware of what accepting this deal means?"

"Yes, your honor. Him and I have spent the majority of the weekend discussing the terms of the plea agreement and he understands the costs of pleading guilty and is willing to take the State's plea."

"Very well. Mr. Houston, please state the terms of agreement for the record."

"Your honor, Mr. Powell is pleading guilty to one count of aggravated domestic assault and one count of aggravated rape on condition he admits his culpability before this court. In doing so, we've agreed to a term of five years for the aggravated domestic assault and five years on the aggravated rape, to be served concurrently at thirty-three percent with the remaining time on parole."

"Mr. Abernathy, is this your understanding of this plea?"

"It is your honor."

"The prosecution has offered, and it would appear the defendant has agreed to the terms set forth before this court. Mr. Powell, if you'll stand. Are you in agreement, fully understanding the plea agreement which has been stated in your presence?" I question.

"Yes, your honor."

"Come forward. Ms. Taylor will you swear him in."

"Please raise your right hand. Do you solemnly swear or affirm the testimony you're about to give will be the truth, the whole truth and nothing but the truth so help you God?"

"Yes."

"For the record, state your full."

"Andre Donte Powell."

"Mr. Powell," I turn to him. "You've been placed under oath for the sake and importance of telling the truth. If you intentionally or unintentionally say anything here under oath which isn't true, you will be charged with committing perjury. In addition, intentionally lying under oath could result in criminal prosecution. In doing so, you forfeit the credit I could give you for pleading guilty and your sentence in this case could be higher. Do you understand all this?"

"Yes, your honor."

"Very well. In speaking to your attorney, were you shown this form?" I hand him the advisement of rights form.

"Yes sir. We went over it this morning."

"Is this your signature?"

"It is." He admits.

"And do you understand by entering these guilty pleas you're altering your rights to appeals as well as giving up certain legal rights which you would have, had you gone through a trial?"

"Yes, your honor."

"Has anyone threatened, pressured or promised you something in agreeing to this plea?"

"No."

"Very well. It has been alleged that on or about September twenty-sixth in the year of 2021, in Memphis, TN, you engaged in the following activity. Count one, you did commit aggravated domestic assault against one, Ms. Ava Gentry. A felony punishable by up to fifteen years in prison. To that charge, how do you plead?"

"Guilty."

"Count two, on or about September twenty-sixth in the year of 2021, in Memphis, TN you knowingly committed the offense of aggravated rape against Ms.

Ava Gentry, a felony punishable by at least fifteen years in prison. To this charge, how do you plead?"

"Guilty."

"Now, I'll ask you to tell the court, in your words, what happened to cause you to be in my courtroom today." I instruct.

He turns in the chair, playing with his hands.

"Mr. Powell, do you need a minute?"

"Your honor, I made a mistake, and it all began the moment I put Ava out. I thought it would be like always. We'd argue then makeup, only this time she didn't come back. I think I took things too far by destroying her belongings. Anyway, I gave her space to cool down and went to her new house to talk to her. I knocked on the door and thought she was ignoring me, so I let myself in. Realizing she wasn't home, I waited. She came home from church, and we argued about her resuming our relationship. She started spouting all this mess about needing better and wanting to be free of me when I was the best thing to ever happen to her." He turns to me. "See, I saved her. She'd be nothing without me and suddenly, she was acting all high and mighty."

"Objection, your honor." Mr. Abernathy hollers.

"Mr. Abernathy, what exactly are you objecting? Your client is admitting what he's already pled guilty too."

"I know, your honor."

"Overruled. Sit down sir. Continue Mr. Powell."

"Ava, I never meant to hurt you."

"Mr. Powell, please address the court, not the galley. What happened after you argued"

"I was walking to the door, and she had this look on her face like she'd won. Before I could stop myself, my hands were around her neck. It was like I was out of my body with no control, and I must have blacked out. The next thing I remember is waking up in the back of the ambulance. They told me I'd raped her and at the time, I didn't consider it rape. Ava was mine which means she belongs to me, including her body.

Since then, I've come to realize I was wrong. I never should have gone to Ava's house. She wanted out and I should have given her what she asked for instead of believing she'd always be there for me like I'd been for her. However, I'm over it, have moved on and forgiven her. I apologize for the pain I inflicted and hope one day she can forgive me too."

"Mr. Powell, did you knowingly inflict bodily harm to your victim?"

"Yes, your honor."

"Do you take responsibility for your actions?"

"Yes, I take full responsibility and I'm ready to do my time and come home."

"Mr. Powell, I'm in agreement with the State's prosecutor in finding you competent to voluntarily give up your rights. I also find your guilt is supported by the facts and your own confession to intentionally afflicting bodily harm to Ms. Ava Gentry. I have to ask a final time. Are you sure you want me to accept your guilty plea?"

"Yes, your honor."

"Very well. This court accepts the defendant's plea to count one and two of the indictment and find him guilty of the offences expressed. Are there any other matters before I rule on sentencing?" I question.

"Yes, your honor." Mr. Houston stands. "Ms. Ava Gentry would like to address the court."

"I'll allow it. Mr. Powell, you may step down."

chapter thirty-nine
Ava

I walk to the stand, sit, and take a deep breath as tears are already starting to form.

"Your honor, thank you for allowing me to speak today. My name is Ava Wilson, once the victim of Andre Powell. I rewrote this statement over and over trying to find the right words to say, only to realize there are none. September 26, 2021, started out as a normal day. It was a Sunday morning and like usual I prepared for church, something I began after the relationship with Mr. Powell ended.

I prayed before leaving the house, attended worship and there was nothing in my spirit signifying the day wouldn't go according to my plans. I'd spoken to God about the contents of my heart and there was nothing there about evil showing up in my home. Yet, it did with a familiar face. The face of the man who I'd shared thirteen years with, even if they weren't all good. Yes, there was a lot of darkness, mental, verbal, financial and emotional abuse during those years, but I never thought he'd inflict this kind of pain upon me.

Your honor, healing from this has been exhausting. Most nights it was hard to sleep without seeing the look in his eyes while he tried to choke the life out of me, every time I closed mine. It was painful due to the bruised ribs, black eyes, and the heartache of knowing he'd rape me in my own home. This has been one of the hardest things I've had to endure, and I've been through a lot in my life.

The first few weeks, I'd see him everywhere, especially when I slept. I had panic attacks and spent nights watching my bedroom door fearful of him returning. He almost destroyed me by instilling this kind of fear. All due to him losing the ability to control me. He wouldn't leave me alone, even though I begged. He believes he saved me when he doesn't have the power.

Yes, I heard him take responsibility for his actions and I hope one day they'll be sincere. However today I don't believe they are. Yet, I need to thank him. Thank you, Andre for not being able to love me, it taught me to love myself and to know what love doesn't look or feel like. It led me to see the man who became my husband." I smile at Levar.

Andre hits the table and I jump. "I knew you were a whore." He yells out. "You marry a random dude after thirteen years?"

I continue looking at Levar.

"Mr. Powell, you will control yourself in my courtroom." Judge Coffee's voice booms. "Do you understand?"

"He understands your honor. I apologize." Mr. Abernathy states pushing him into the chair.

"You may continue Ms. Wilson."

"The fear showed me I'm stronger than I believed. The pain taught me how to breathe especially when it hurts. The struggle to live beyond what you did saved me, pushing me closer to God. You almost destroyed me, but you failed. Since you did, I get the chance to restart. Your honor, he deserves the years he'll spend in prison and hopefully he'll use the time to become a better human being before he ruins the life of anyone else. Thank you."

I walk pass without even looking at him.

"Mr. Powell, please stand."

We all wait for the judge to speak.

"Mr. Powell, although this court has accepted your guilty plea, I find the sentencing of this agreement to be considerably lower than what your crime and actions deserve. You intentionally harmed another human being for deciding to want better for her life and what's to say you won't do the same the next time. Your actions, although I don't believe were premeditated were impulsive and destructive and I am well within my rights to change the sentence."

I look at Jamia.

"For count one, aggravated domestic assault, I am imposing a sentence of six years served at 35% and six years of supervised parole. For count two, aggravated rape, eight years served at 35% and six years of supervised parole. Each sentence to be served consecutively for a total of fourteen years. At a serve time of 35%, this equals to 4.9 years after which you'll be eligible for twelve years of supervised parole. In addition, I'm also ordering anger management, conflict resolution and behavioral classes. Mr. Powell, due to my imposing a different sentence than what was agreed upon, you now have the right to choose to withdraw your guilty plea and move forward with trial or accept the modified deal. I'll give you time to think about it and talk it over with your attorney. We'll reconvene at 9:00 AM tomorrow morning.

"What just happened?" I ask Jamia when we reach the hall.

"Judges have discretion in sentencing even with a plea bargain and he's well within his right to impose a different sentence. Now, it's up to Andre whether he wants to take the modified agreement or go to trial."

"This is all your fault, you bitch." Katrina screams coming towards us. "The lies and filth you spewed in your little speech added two more years to his sentence. I should have made you suffer when I had the chance."

"Lady, you need to find something productive to do." Levar steps in front of me.

"Who are you?" she looks him up and down.

"Ava's husband and can be your worst nightmare."

"I'm not afraid of y'all." She yells causing a deputy to rush over.

"Ma'am, you need to calm down or I'll have to ask you to leave."

"Me? She's the one who needs to leave. My husband's life is being ruined, not hers."

"Frankly, I don't care." He tells her. "Either control yourself or get out of my courthouse. Do you understand?"

She nods swiping tears from her face.

"You're going to pay for this." She angrily whispers once he walks away.

"No sis, I prayed for this. Katrina, you sat in the same courtroom as the rest of us while dude confessed to what he did to me, yet you're either stupid or," I pause. "No, it's plain stupidity. Nothing else will make it hard for you to comprehend what you heard out of his mouth."

"He lied to protect you."

"The only person I need protection from is him and apparently you. Katrina, he's playing you and I pray you spend the time he's gone, getting the help you need."

"I'm not you sweetie."

"Really? You're probably cooking his meals, paying all his bills, and giving him sex whenever he requests. Your new hairdo is due to him although he'll act as if he doesn't like it. Every time you have an argument, you end up apologizing even though he's the one wrong and everything has to be about him at all times. Oh, has he promised to pay you back once his money comes in?"

She doesn't say anything.

I laugh. "How many times has he left the house to give you time to think about what you've done?"

"He's not like—you don't know him."

"Neither do you and you can continue with the fake social media pages. They don't bother me. You'll run out of time before I allow you to occupy anymore space in my mind. Good luck though."

"Babe, let's go." Levar grabs my hand.

Walking out of the courthouse, I stop and look at him.

"What?"

"It's the "Ava's husband and can be your worst nightmare," for me." I mock in a deep tone. "Mane, I'm going to put on some Luther and feed you butter roll in my Red Bottoms tonight."

chapter forty
Andre

Sitting in a room inside the courthouse, I'm thumbing through pictures of me and Ava, remembering the times when things were good between us. I can't believe she married some dude.

"Why are you looking at pictures of her?" Katrina asks, startling me.

"Why are you looking over my shoulder?" I lock the phone, sliding it into my pocket.

"Do you still love her?"

"No."

"Then why do you look like you've lost your best friend?"

"I'm angry." I lash out. "My entire life is over and you're worried if I love Ava. Look at where I am, Trina. Loving her or not, it won't change my outcome. I have to decide whether to take five years of prison time or risk going to trial and you want to argue. Sometimes you need to think before you speak foolishness. I have enough on my plate and if this is what you're going to do, then leave. It's not like I have anybody else. My own mother didn't show up."

"You have me." She rushes over.

"Do I or are you here to make Ava mad?"

"Forget Ava. This isn't about her. I'm here for you."

The door opens and my lawyer walks in.

"Good morning. Am I interrupting?"

"No, come in."

"Dre were you able to get the cashier's check to cover the bounced payment? My boss isn't happy about us representing you without being paid."

"Bruh, if only you lawyered like you ask for money. Boo, did you get the cashier's check for me?" I ask Katrina.

"Yes. Here."

"Thanks." I kiss her forehead. "Now, go."

"What?"

"Things with us are over. You don't honestly think you and I will be anything once I'm released, do you?"

"After all I've done for you?"

"All we've done for each other, sweetie."

"What have you done for me? Huh? You liar." She hits me with her purse. "I should have killed you when I had the chance."

"Yeah, you should have. Too late now though. Good luck to you."

She straightens her posture, smoothing down her shirt. "It may be for you, but not for those you love. Oh, and Andre. Don't drop the soap."

The door closes and he turns to me.

"Dude, if this crazy chick tries to kill me because of you." Langston says.

"Relax. She's harmless. Anyway, she said those I love. I don't love you."

"Thank God. What am I doing with this?" he refers to the check.

"Take care of Crystal's case. She doesn't deserve to go to jail for helping me. She's already lost her job."

"I'll do everything I can for her."

"Thanks. Here." I hand him my phone. "I don't want Katrina getting access to this. I also hired a management company to rent out my house while I'm gone. You have all the paperwork and access to my financials. Please be sure to take care of my affairs Lang. Don't have me getting released, homeless and broke."

"What about your mother?"

"What about her? She's grown."

"Say no more. I got you. You ready?"

"As ready as a man being led to the electric chair."

———

"All rise," the clerk announces. "Twelfth District Court is in session. The honorable Judge Linnell Coffee presiding. Please be seated."

"Good morning. On yesterday, we adjourned with the matter of whether Mr. Powell would like to accept the amended sentencing or rescind his plea. Mr. Abernathy, has your client reached a decision?"

"Yes, your honor. After much consideration, Mr. Powell has decided to take the plea."

I hear Ava exhale. Looking back at her, she has tears falling, mouthing *Thank you Jesus.*

Katrina clears her throat. I turn back to face the judge who restates the terms of the deal.

"Mr. Powell, please stand. You are hereby remanded to the Tennessee Department of Correction to serve out the time in accordance with the agreed upon deal. It is this court's hope you will spend this time getting the help you need to be a productive citizen for when you are released back into society."

"Your honor, if I may?" Langston stands.

"Go ahead."

"Mr. Powell is requesting to be housed close to the city as he has an ailing mother who'd like to visit him."

"Mr. Abernathy, I can only make a recommendation. You know it isn't up to me where your client will spend his term."

"Yes sir, thank you your honor. A recommendation would be great."

"Good luck to you Mr. Powell. Court adjourned."

Katrina

"He thinks I'll be dismissed after everything I've done for him. I jeopardized my entire life for you, punk!" I scream inside the car. "My savings account is depleted after giving you the last of it. I'm behind on my mortgage. I was fired from my job, and you think it's over. You think you're going to screw me." I laugh. "We'll see buddy boy. We will see."

I get ready to pull off when I see Ava walking out smiling.

I put my car in drive, easing out of the parking space.

chapter forty-one
Ava

"Ava, hey. It's been a while. How have you been?" Dr. Greene asks beginning our session.

"I got married a few weeks ago."

"Okay." She stutters. "Wasn't expecting that. How do you feel?"

"Lighter." I admit playing with my ring.

"As in weight lifted or the opposite of darkness?"

"Both." I admit. "Dr. Greene, Levar has been a constant in my life and all he asked for in return was a healing me. Not healed, but in the process because he understands it takes time. He was patient and told me to come get him when I was ready." I chuckle. "I did and the next day we were married. One of the best days of my life. Although, I will confess. I'm a little scared. What if I mess things up?"

"What if you do? What if he does? Nobody is perfect, and messes can be cleaned up. Here's my advice. Make plans for the potential but enjoy the present."

"Make plans for the potential but enjoy the present?" I repeat questioningly. "What do you mean?"

"Ava, there's a potential for "rainy days." However, you don't stop enjoying the sunshine while you wait on the possibility of rain showing up. You enjoy the moment. In other words, be happy with the happiness you've been gifted. Focusing on the what ifs and worrying about what might happen will have you making unwise choices while missing the things you've prayed for."

"I'm trying."

"Are you having second thoughts about the marriage?"

"No, it's just." I exhale.

"You can be honest here. This is a safe place."

"Dr. Greene, everything between me and Levar happened so fast and I'm not questioning the genuineness of his heart, I'm questioning mine. All I've ever had was pain."

"It's all you've ever had, past tense. Ava, you can attend sessions with me every day of the week and I can drill it into you that you deserve love. You can even experience authentic love from a man who'll be patient and willing to love you while you're healing. However, until your mentality change, you'll always end back at this point of questioning if you deserve it."

"How do I get out of my own way?"

"By changing. Let's say you're driving on a two-lane highway. The lane you happen to be in has you stuck behind a person driving way under the speed limit. You have somewhere to be and if you stay stuck, you won't make it. What do you do?"

"Change lanes."

"Ava, you may have physically left the relationship with Andre, but mentally you're still there."

I look away.

"Ava?"

"You're right. Andre was sentenced yesterday, and I thought I'd be relieved. Instead, I feel like I've experienced death. Which is crazy because on my ride here, I thought about the many times I was so naïve and foolish for Andre. He was so good at manipulating. I would have jeopardized my life for a Negro who wouldn't have cared if mine ended. I believed everything he said even when I knew it wasn't true and nobody could tell me differently. God knows I was a fool. Yet, a part of me is sad and it makes me angry to feel sorry for him. Isn't that silly?" I ask Dr. Greene while wiping the falling tears.

"No. This is the cycle of control abusers use to keep you tethered to them. It's also not uncommon to love the abuser enough to fight for them. This is the CPTSD and trauma bonds we've talked about. Being bound to an abuser intoxicates you. It'll have you willingly doing anything for the love you think they give, never stopping to weigh the cost. Sometimes people don't survive. Other times, they do. Ava, you survived, and you shouldn't feel guilty about crying. Yesterday marked the closing of something you shared thirteen years of your life with and it's natural to grieve the loss even if it was bad. Now, you need to forgive yourself for the decisions you made while in trauma."

"I'm trying. Yet, he doesn't deserve my tears. He hurt me and afterwards, him and his girlfriend made my life hell. They don't get to make me cry too."

"Why do your tears have to be for them? Why can't they wash away the residue pain left behind? Why can't they signify death to what has tried to destroy you? Why can't they be watering the ground for everything good you've been praying for over the years? We seem to think people have control over the meaning of our tears. Our tears belong to us and no matter what has caused us to cry, we decide their value.

See, Bible tells us in Psalm 126 around verse five, *"Those who plant in tears will harvest with shouts of joy. They weep as they go to plant their seed, but they sing as they return with the harvest."* Ava, for every dark moment you had to walk through, you were planting seeds. For every tear you shed, you're watering the ground. Now, you're about to reap the harvest you didn't realize was growing because you had to cry. You thought your tears were for nothing, when they have power, you just needed to let them work."

She comes over handing me tissue.

"You have a harvest of joy, laughing, and an armload of blessings waiting for you to reap, although you may have to cry to get it. Bishop Morton said it best. Your tears are just temporary relief and release of the pain, sorrow, and grief. And a little crying out is alright. So cry then get up."

I let out a wail stretching my arms out. After a few minutes, I hear music playing.

Though it seems it's delayed, delayed is not denied. The wait is only has only given you strength to stand in the fight. Be encouraged my brother, sister don't give up. Your tears have paid off for you. I know it hurts sometimes, you're still on God's mind. It might seem like He's gone but He'll show up on time. Please don't you worry, it's working out for your good. Your tears have paid off for you."

"Whew. I didn't know I had that penned up." I tell her finally able to speak.

"You'll be surprised at the things we can pack away unintentionally. Which is why crying isn't all bad."

"Thank you, Dr. Greene."

"Let's pray. Father, in your infinite wisdom, thank you. Thank you for the tears we have to shed knowing they're watering seeds we've planted in despair. God, we may not always understand why we have to cry, but we'll trust in the power of our tears. Like David says in your word, you keep count of our sorrows and collect our tears in your bottle which lets me know, you're close to us when we suffer. Thank you, God. Now God, continue to cover Ava, protecting her from evil and giving her strength to keep the promises she's made to you in secret. The promise of removing the woe is me from her vocabulary and to see light even when surrounded by darkness. Father, let her enjoy the blessings of today and be happy with the happiness she's been gifted. In Your name we pray, amen."

"Amen."

chapter forty-two

Getting home, I have the house to myself. I drop my purse on the table and kick off my shoes, walking around the living room.

"My tears have power. God, I declare with every tear I have to shed they'll water my harvest of happiness."

I fall to my knees beginning to sing.

"Withholding nothing." I repeat. "Lord I surrender all to you. Everything I give to you. Withholding nothing. I give myself away, I give myself away so you can use me." I moan. "All I want is you. Oh God. All I want is you. Here I am to worship. Here I am to bow down. Here I am to say that you're my God. You're altogether lovely. Altogether worthy. Altogether wonderful to me. Here I am to worship. Here I am to bow down. Here I am to say that you're my God. You're altogether lovely. Altogether worthy. Altogether wonderful to me."

I wrap my arms around myself.

"Hallelujah. Lord thank you for keeping your hands on me. God, it was nobody but you who could save a wretch like me. You brought me through dangers, kept me when I didn't deserve to be kept, spared my life, fought battles I never had to lift a finger in, and I didn't lose my mind. Then you'd lead me to happiness I didn't think I deserved. You sent me a family who loves me despite what I've been through. When I showed up battered and bruised, they didn't judge instead they were willing to bandage my wounds. They believed in me more than I did myself. Oh, but you didn't stop there. You, being God, crafted and shaped a man just for me and you did mighty good. Thank you, Father. When I thought it was over, you made a way. When darkness and sin had me wrapped tight, you freed me. Oh God."

A wail erupts from within me, and I begin to moan.

Levar

I rush into the house when I hear Ava cry out, calling her name. Abruptly stopping when I see her in the living room floor eyes closed, and arms outstretched. I stand there watching as she moans and rock in worship to God. I begin to speak in tongue asking God to destroy every barrier keeping her from being healed.

When she bends, forehead touching the floor, I go and kneel beside her.

She jumps.

"It's me." I tell her.

"I'm sorry."

"Babe, don't ever apologize for needing to worship." I sit, pulling her into me. "This is a safe place and can be turned into your altar at any time. When you pour out, God pours in."

She relaxes into me, and I tighten the hold.

"I got you." I assure her. After a few minutes, I begin to sing. "I believe the storm will soon be over. I believe the rain will go away. I believe that you can make it through it. I believe it's already done."

We sit in the quietness of the room for a while until she sits up.

"Thank you." She tells me.

"For what?"

"This and for trusting God concerning me."

"Ava, you're my wife and I'll do whatever it takes to ensure you're good. Even if it's sitting in the middle of the living room for hours." I laugh.

She stands, reaching out her hand to help me up.

"I love you Levar and I'm grateful I get the chance to show you for however long God ordains."

"I love you too and I pray everything broken in this room tonight will never find its way back to you. I pray you'll finally see yourself the way I do. Beautiful, courageous, bold, and worthy. I pray every chain once holding you is destroyed. I pray every bond with self-doubt is burned by Heaven's fire. I pray God's peace and protection over you. I pray your mind will be forever changed for the good work of God, in Heaven and on Earth. I also pray our union will be bonded by God's hand because of this moment. You are my wife in whom I'm well pleased and I seal this with amen and a kiss."

"Lord, I don't know what I did to deserve him, but thank you."

"Now, about them red bottoms, butter roll and Luther you promised."

chapter forty-three
Ava

Levar and I walk into Gracewood Baptist Church.

"Oh my God. Tobias, get out here." Lady Ruthie yells into the sanctuary. "Ava, we've been trying to get in touch with you. The last time you were here, you blessed our church in such a way."

"Young lady, we can never repay you for the tithe you sowed into us. The money you graciously shared helped us do a lot of repairs around here. We're forever grateful." Pastor Tobias tells me. "If there's anything we can do for you, don't hesitate to ask."

He hugs me before returning to the sanctuary.

"Are you and your beautiful family staying for service?" Ruthie asks.

"Yes ma'am. This is my husband Levar, and these young ladies are our godchildren, Bailey, and Briley. Everyone, this is First Lady Ruthie."

"Well, come on in. We're about to start."

"Um ma'am, how much did you give the last time you were here?" Levar whispers.

"Not much. Only ten thousand."

"Only? Girl, had they known you were coming, there would have been a red carpet out." He laughs and I push him through the door.

Thirty minutes later, after a soul stirring rendition of Glory, Glory, Hallelujah, Pastor Tobias is doing his good preaching from Acts 14.

"These people punished Paul by stoning which was a horrible way to die. Can you imagine the heart of a person who would hurl a rock at your naked body with so much strength that it pierces the skin causing blunt trauma? Blunt trauma is an impactful force causing contusions, abrasions, lacerations, internal hemorrhages, bone fractures, as well as death. These same people who begged Paul to preach are now inflicting wounds to his body. Not stopping until they thought he was dead. Then as his limp body lay on the ground, they drag him out of the city, discarding him like trash. And somebody in this place, you've never been stoned but the hatred you've received felt just as bad.

Those who turned on you or believed the lies when they should know your character. People who said they loved you, but now their words feel like stones piercing your flesh. Some of you, it's family members who've done and said hurtful things and all you can do is stand there as their stones scar your skin. It's not because you've done anything to die over, they're jealous of the favor without knowing the hell you had to go through to survive long enough to see your seeds pay off. They see your glory but won't sit long enough to hear the story. Yet, the nappy headed Negroes got the audacity to throw stones.

If that ain't bad enough, they got the nerve to cry over your body. It's cool, I ain't mad at you playa. Do what you want to me because when you've done your worse, all I need is the believers to gather. You can hurt me, lie on me, scandalize my name, but all I need is the believers to gather. After Paul was stoned, dragged out and threw away believing to be dead, Bible says in Acts 14:20, "*But as the believers gathered around him, he got up.*"

"Preach sir." I say standing from my seat.

"Somebody needs to let your enemy know. You may have wished me dead, smiled when you saw me down, picked out your dress for the funeral, rehearsed your song, ordered the flowers, and prepared the obituaries. However, I came to serve notice, I ain't dead yet. The believers gathered, and I got up. The believers gathered and the blood began to work. In other words, his heart started to beat again which made blood start flowing sending oxygen to every corner of the body. Brain started functioning, transmitting to the mind the ability to feel pain, sights, sounds and smell. Lungs began to work causing him to inhale and exhale, extracting oxygen from the intake of air.

The open wounds started to heal. His labored breathing became steady, and strength returned to its rightful place. Why? The believers gathered. See, some of you when you go through hell, get sick, find yourself in sin, or facing a storm you run from the church. When truth is, you need the believers."

"I need the believers." I repeat.

Once service is over, we spend a few minutes talking to Pastor, Lady Ruthie, and a few members of the church. Inside the truck, the girls picked Huey's for lunch. Walking out after putting my name on the list, I hear someone call my name.

"Jack."

"Wow, you look amazing." He says like it's a shock.

"New beginnings will do that for you. What's up?"

"How have things been with you?"

"Dude, we aren't friends. Say what you need, my family is waiting."

"You have every right to be angry at me. I was a coward for not standing up for you when I should have. A decision I've regretted every day since."

"Cool. Happy Sunday."

"Wait, please. After everything happened, I quit working for Ruthie & Associates. The job and my father were draining the life out of me. So much that I tried to commit suicide. It didn't work, obviously but it gave me the courage to stand up for myself. Ava, I truly am sorry for the drama I caused, and I hope one day you'll be able to forgive me."

He turns to walk away.

"Jack, wait. I do forgive you otherwise the anger will reside within me. Truthfully, I'm glad you lied. Being fired opened the door for the blessings I now get to enjoy. A new career with Small Sticks and a wonderful husband who loves me. I guess I should thank you. So, thank you Jack. I pray you'll finally find happiness and peace you've been longing for."

I get inside the truck. "Was that Jack Kingston."

"Yeah. He wanted to apologize for lying on me."

"Dang, I should have thanked him. His lies led to my good thang."

"I did." I smile. "You're welcome."

"My girl." He holds up his hand for a fist bump.

chapter forty-four

I'm in my office when there's a tap on the door.

"Mrs. Ava, your 3 PM appointment is here."

I look up to see Marble.

"You're kidding me?"

"Ma'am?" Jayla questions looking from me to her.

"Thank you, Jayla. I'll take it from here."

She gives one last glance then closes the door.

"We need to talk."

"Why would I need to talk to you, Ms. Lillian Barkley of Livewell Medical?" Referring to the name she booked under.

"I knew you wouldn't see me otherwise."

"You're right. During the entire thirteen years I was with your son, you never had anything to say to me. Keep it that way and show yourself out."

"Water under the bridge. You seem to be doing well." She picks up the picture of me and Levar.

I snatch it from her as she takes a seat in front of my desk.

"Mabel, please say whatever it is and leave. I've had enough of you and your family."

She rolls her eyes at my mispronouncing her name. "Did you know Andre was a whiny baby? He cried up until he was like four. Couldn't take the boy nowhere and God knows nobody would keep him. So, I started leaving him home alone or giving him a down South beating like my mother gave me. He finally learned his lesson. Although he was a slow learner."

"What's the point in telling me this?"

"Anyway, I still loved his big head ass and by the time he turned ten, I'd whipped him into shape."

"Whipped him into shape?"

"Yeah. I taught him the rules of life. One, you always come first. Two, get them before they get you. Three, be quick and don't catch feelings. He was good at it too. He'd find vulnerable women. I'd take care of the men. Looks really didn't matter, only their account balance. We'd get'em sprung then drain their bank accounts and be on to the next. Oh, it was fun. Until you. I couldn't understand why you. You didn't have nothing going for yourself, but he was like a dog. Had the smell of your pee in his nostrils and needed to mark his territory. I hated you for it."

"How am I to blame for your grown son making his own decisions? I didn't put a gun to his head."

"No. It was worse. He fell in love with you." She dry heaves. "Love. Ugh."

"Lady, and I use the terms loosely, Andre doesn't love me. He wanted to control me."

"Same thing." She waves her hand. "When he put you out, I was ecstatic to finally get my boy back. But no, he couldn't let you go. Ruining my plans to buy a house on an island somewhere. Shoot, I'm too old to be hoeing. Do you know how hard you have to work to get niggas to part with their money when you're my age? The jaws ain't like they used to be. Although having no teeth gets them every time."

"You can't be serious. One, you're disgusting and two, get out of my office."

She laughs. "You haven't heard the reason why I'm here."

"Other than to annoy me? No thanks." I lift my finger to call Jayla.

"It's about Katrina." She asserts. "You may want to listen."

"What does she have to do with this?"

"Okay." She exhales. "We met at the Labor Day thingy. I saw the way she was looking at Andre and knew she'd be easy to use. It didn't hurt she had money either."

"How did you know she had money?"

"She had a few drinks and told me. She had no idea I was his mother. Apparently, she had an accident some years ago which resulted in a huge settlement. Anyway, a couple years ago he helped her after she was robbed, carjacked, or something. Sound familiar?"

"You're pushing it."

She laughs. "She followed him on social media, liked and commented on anything he posted but she stayed in her place. I think she was trying to figure out how to get rid of you, but she didn't admit it. After her and Andre started talking, I reintroduced myself. In my defense, she was only supposed to take his mind off you. I thought with you out the way, Andre would come to his senses. Then the dummy went and attacked you. All that head and no sense. He got it from his pappy, God bless him."

"Marble." I say to get her back on track. "What does this have to do with me?"

"When I realized she hated you as much as me, I used her to make you suffer."

"Like I hadn't suffered enough. Woman, your son attacked me."

"You're right. In hindsight, the plan was stupid, and I allowed myself to be led astray by this old flesh. Praise God for deliverance."

"Deliverance? All you mother—Jesus. All y'all need help."

"It was only a few drugs and without a criminal history, you would have gotten probation. But her weak brother couldn't even do it right. So, we came up with the harassment and stalking. I didn't count on your lawyer being good."

"Do you hear yourself?" I yell. "You could have ruined my life."

"You're being dramatic, it wasn't that serious. Anyway hun, I won't hold you. I got a plane to catch. I just wanted to apologize and tell you to be on the lookout for Katrina. Sis doesn't have all her screws. If you know what I mean. Good luck to you."

"Good luck. Screw your luck." I pick up my coffee cup and throw the remaining liquid in her face. "How dare you wobble your Thomas, the tank looking self in here acting like what you've done is nothing. Your son's actions are what put him where he is, not mine. Yet, I've had to pay the cost. Marble, you better be glad I'm working on my salvation, or I'd gladly go to jail again. This time for elderly abuse." I go over and open the door. "Get out of my office and I hope you, Andre and Katrina share a special place in hell."

"We probably will, but I don't plan on going any time soon."

"Uh, Ava?" Larissa says walking pass Marble who has coffee dripping.

"Andre's mammy."

"Say less."

A few minutes later, Levar is standing at the door. "Ava Justine Wilson. You did not throw coffee in that lady's face."

"I sure did then repented. I'm sick of them acting like my feelings don't matter. Sitting in her with a wig from the beauty supply, looking like a wet poodle. Baby, she was the one who sent Katrina after me. I hope they burn in hell."

"Okay. Okay." He comes over. "Calm down. Andre can't hurt you and God will deal with them. I only have one question."

"What?"

"Did you get a picture of the poodle?"

We both laugh.

"Seriously babe. I'm proud of you for standing up for yourself and I hope it's the last you hear from either of them."

"From your lips to God's ears."

"Now, can we get out of here and enjoy our honeymoon?"

"Can." I quickly close my laptop, grab my purse, and follow him out.

chapter forty-five

The following day, we're waiting for the plane to take off when my phone vibrates with a text from June.

June – Tru's Mommy: You've got to see this.

I click it and a video begins to play.

"Memphis Police have released the identity of a woman witnesses say was pushed out of a moving car on I-240 and then ran over by multiple vehicles. A spokesperson for the coroner's office identified the deceased as 68-year-old Marble Jefferson who was pronounced dead at the scene. The suspect fled and was later found at a local motel where she refused to surrender. Onlookers captured the following video. Be aware, what you're about to see is graphic."

I pause it and touch Levar's arm, telling him what happened and giving him one of my Air Pods. Raising the phone, I resume playing.

"Ma'am, please put the gun down and let's talk about this."

"There's nothing to talk about. She deserved to die. She and her son took everything from me. Everything. Y'all should be thanking me for ridding the world of her. The only reason her son is still alive is because he's in

jail. His bitch ass deserves to die too." She yells through the open door."

"We understand, but you shouldn't die over it. Please put the gun down and surrender."

"You want me to surrender? Okay. Sure. I'll surrender."

"She's coming out." An officer screams. "Hold your fire."

Katrina steps out looking wired on something with her hair and clothes disheveled.

"Place the gun on the ground and raise your hands." A man shouts.

She looks at the gun then at them. "I never saw this for my life. I should have listened to her. They drained me of everything. My dignity, peace, happiness, and money. And she had the nerve to laugh."

"Ma'am, drop the gun."

"She laughed in my face. Man, I should have listened. Tell Ava I'm sorry." She points the gun at the officers, pulling the trigger causing them to fire back. The video stops with her falling to the ground.

My hand flies to my mouth as we look at each other.

"I didn't see that coming." Levar says. "Are you okay?"

"Wow. I—I, wow. Lord knows I wish she would have listened instead of losing her life this way. I only hope her soul rest in peace."

He grabs my hand. "Lord, we pray for the souls of Katrina and Marble, hoping they'll be received into your care and will rest in peace. Amen."

"Amen." I put my Air Pod back in, play Promises by Maverick City and reply to June with a shock face emoji.

June – Tru's Mommy: I know right, and she took Marble on out of here. Lawd, may they rest in peace. On a brighter note, the men of Memphis are safe, and you can enjoy your honeymoon.

Me: Praise Him. I'll text you when we land.

———————

Two nights later, I come out of the bathroom of our villa to Levar dressed in a tuxedo.

"You look amazing." He tells me.

"Thank you. My husbae picked it out." I spin to show off the white fitted, floor length dress with a split up the front and the shoes he gifted me for Christmas. My hair is braided and pinned into a bun.

"He knows his wife. Shall we?" he holds out his arm leading me out to the private beach.

"Babe. Oh my God. What is all this?"

There are lights. flowers and candles all over.

"You remember the bet we made when you cooked? You won and I promised you a night of dancing."

"It's beautiful." I fan my eyes to not cry my lashes off.

He goes over pressing something on his phone and Teddy Pendergrass' *When Somebody Love You Back* begins. Thirty minutes later after a mixture of R&B, Blues and Line Dancing, we sit for a catered dinner of seafood and wine.

"What are you thinking?" Levar asks.

"I never want to lose this."

"The traveling?"

"No. Traveling is cool, but I'm talking about true happiness, fun, laughter and making of memories. I lost a lot of time in darkness and regret, focusing on things I'd endured instead of what I survived. I get we're going to go through things, but even when life gets chaotic, can we make a vow to always take a moment to enjoy the light?"

He reaches across the table for my hand.

"Ava Justine Wilson—

"What is it with you and calling my whole name?" I laugh.

"It makes it sound more official. Anyway, stop interrupting my mushy moment woman. Now." He clears his throat. "Ava Justine Wilson, I love you and will do whatever it takes to make you happy."

"No babe, I don't want that."

"What do you mean?"

"If you spend all your time making me happy, where does your happiness come in?"

"From you."

"Levar, I love you and I plan to give you all I have the capacity too. However, every piece of your happiness cannot solely be dependent on me and vice versa. When that happens, we'll turn what we used to enjoy into a weight and regret. If I've learned anything on this healing journey, it's you also need self happiness. So, here's what I suggest. While we're creating a space where we dance to the beat of our music, laugh to our personal jokes, form our own traditions, and make memories, let's not forget the personal time we need. This way, when you're happy with self, you can also be happy with me. Deal?"

He stands up.

"Levar?"

He goes over to his phone. A few minutes later, the song *Where Have You Been* by Rihanna plays and I laugh.

Coming back, he pulls me up. "You have a deal."

chapter forty-six

A couple weeks later, Levar and I are headed to the closing of our home after leaving the hospital. June delivered a healthy, eight-pound four-ounce, Tru Abigail Carson on April 29, 2022, at 10:17 AM.

"Did you see how perfect she is?" I ask Levar while thumbing through all the pictures I took. "Man, I'm so happy for Grant and June. They've been waiting for this a long time."

"Delayed does not mean denial."

"Amen indeed." I reply looking at the unknown number on my phone.

"Hello." I answer. "Speaking. What can I do for you Mr. Abernathy? Against my better judgment, sure." I put the phone on speaker. "You've got to hear this." I tell Levar.

"Go ahead." Abernathy says.

"Ava, thank you for taking my call. I know I had no right to have Lang call you, but after learning of the horrible way my mother died, I realized my part in this. Man." He sighs. "I messed up. Had I been honest with you from the beginning, maybe none of this would have happened. Ava, in some way, I did love you although I didn't go about showing it. One of the worst mistakes I made was not being there when our son died. Instead, I blamed you. Truth is, I never wanted children because well, I didn't want another version of me. Which is why I had a vasectomy afterwards."

"A vasectomy? So, you knew Katrina wasn't pregnant? You dirty sucker."

I'm sorry. Ava, I'm truly sorry and I hope the man you're with can finally give you the happiness you deserve."

"I do. Every day and night." Levar states.

Andre clears his throat. "I know I have no reason to ask but—

"But what?" I ask.

"The phone hung up." Abernathy states. "Mrs. Wilson, with the passing of Andre's mother, he needs someone to be the executor of her estate. He has no other family and would like you to do it until he's released."

"Sir, I thought you was smarter than this and the mere fact you dialed my number for this foolishness is cause to get cussed out. Do not, under any circumstance, call my phone again. All y'all stupid." I hang up and block his number. "The nerve of them. Did he actually think I'd say yes? Executor of his mammy's estate. I bet not."

Levar touches my hand. "Breathe. He has no more control over your life and he's not about to ruin our day. We're going to close on our home, stop and get a bottle of champagne and an air mattress from Walmart."

"Air mattress?"

"How else can we christen every room before moving in?"

"Oh Mr. Wilson, I like the way you think."

June 19, 2022

"It has been a long year." I admit to our family in the backyard of our home. "Last year, I never would have imagined I'd be standing here surrounded by love, hope, joy and light. However, we decided to do this celebration today, on Juneteenth because of its symbolism of freedom. Today y'all, I can declare I am free. I made a promise to God to not spend another moment with woe in my vocabulary and I promised myself, I'd get up. The times when life hits me and it hurts, I'll get up. Every time the enemy attempts to knock me down or the times I may happen to fall, I'll get up. I'll get up because that's where my life and hope is. Y'all, I'm grateful and I couldn't let this moment pass without thanking each of you. My husband. I'll never get tired of saying that."

They laugh.

"I'll never tire of hearing it." Levar stands coming over to take my hand. "Ava, I told you one day I'd stand before our family and friends, under the anointing of God reciting vows I don't plan to break. I meant it. I said I'd tell them how God created you for me. He perfectly crafted your spirit to complement mine, your hand fits my hand and God sculpted you with the right measure of curves which fit snug into the crease of my body. It didn't matter what we'd experienced, or how long it took for you to say yes."

He clears his throat causing everybody to laugh.

"It was the right amount of time." He smiles. "Seriously, nothing could destroy the plans God has for us. You are my good thang and I'm grateful, every day, I get to wake up and every night I have to lay down beside you. Thank you for saying yes."

"Aw." The women say.

"Levar, I'm so glad God knows us better than we know ourselves. Meeting you, I was not in a place to see love and I almost destroyed it. Yet, you waited. You never asked for anything physical or materialistic. You waited. Yes, I made things harder, yet you were willing to be patient. When I pushed, you pulled. When I shut the door, you knocked. When I wanted to argue, you'd kiss me on the forehead and tell me to call you when I got home." I chuckle through tears. "And I would. When you knew I needed time, you told me and when I came back to get my man, you were there. Only a man after God's heart can love like this. Babe, I love you and plan to spend each day showing you."

"You may now kiss the bride." Pastor Tobias says.

When Levar releases me, I turn to everybody.

"Y'all." I say with tears falling. "I need this. I need each of you. Grant, June, and my baby Tru, I love y'all for always being willing. I'm leaving the statement open ended because there's too much to list. You all stepped into my life and there was never a second thought. Thank you. To Ma Nellie, Pop, Levitra, Michael, Larissa, Josiah, Naomi, Bailey, and Briley. God couldn't have created a better set of family if I'd written out the requirements myself. Each of you have something I need, and I thank you for receiving and loving me.

And to my newest Pastor Tobias and Lady Ruthie. Experiencing God and Gracewood Baptist has been a blessing to my life, and I thank God for leading me to a church home." I pause to control the emotions. "I was almost destroyed, but God let me live. He saved me and

I have to believe it was to experience this. Here's to the healing power of family and friends. May the grace of our God cover and protect the sanctity of this forever. May we always find time to be. May we make memories and enjoy the light."

"Amen." We all say.

Thank you for taking this journey with Ava. Although this is a fictional story, I pray it has helped you in some way. Maybe Ava's story isn't yours, but you too have gone through some things in your life. Yet, my prayer for you is the same …

Father, help the sister and/or brother who's found themselves in darkness. God, help the parts of them yet to heal. Help the ones who have been almost destroyed by abuse, self-doubt, sabotage, lies, hurt, pain, physical, emotional, mental, financial, or sexual abuse. God, deliver them, giving them strength to not return to what they've had to pray themselves out of. Father, let their tears water the harvest they'll soon reap. And God, if they have you on hold, please don't hang up because they need you. When they return, forgive their sins, and hear their prayer. In the name of Jesus, amen.

As always with every book, I wouldn't be Lakisha if I didn't leave you with this. If you need help, get it. Seek a licensed therapist because therapy isn't a bad thing. You deserve to be healed, happy and whole. You deserve to be free. You deserve to find you.

If you don't know God and desire to, say this. "God, forgive me of any sin, removing anything distracting and detouring me from getting to you. Come into my heart as my Lord and Savior, taking control of my life. Help me to walk in you, guiding my footsteps daily by the power of the Holy Spirit. Thank you, God, for saving me and answering my prayer. Amen."

I am in no way affiliated with the companies and websites listed below. I am providing them as a source of help for those who may need it. Any kind of abuse is abuse.

Find the courage to ask for help.
HELP IS AVAILABLE

If you're in Memphis, contact **Montoyia McGowan,**
LCSW

https://www.stoppingthechase.com/ |
901.273.3485

https://www.thehotline.org/
National Domestic Violence Hotline
1.800.799.7233
National Sexual Assault Hotline
1.800.656.4673
National Suicide Prevention Lifeline
1.800.273.8255
Find an African American Therapist:
https://www.psychologytoday.com/us/therapists/afr
ican-american
Black Virtual Therapist Directory
https://www.beam.community/bvtn
Therapy for Black Girls
https://therapyforblackgirls.com/

Again, thank you for taking the time to read and support Almost Destroyed. I pray you enjoyed it. If you did, please leave a review, post it on social media (tag me) and share it with friends and family. If you're a member of a book club and would like to feature this book, email me at authorlakisha@gmail.com as I'd love to be a part of the discussion.

Oh, allow me to shout out some black businesses.

Chicks and Cigars, owned and operated by Laquisha Rucker. Visit her at https://chicksandcigars.com/ and try a rum or cherry flavored cigar.

Biscuits and Jams. Check them out at https://biscuitsandjams.com/ or 5806 Stage Rd, Bartlett, TN 38134. Tell Chef Mo, Lakisha sent you.

As always, I'm grateful each time you support me. If this is your first or twentieth time reading a book by me, THANK YOU! If we haven't connected on social media, what are you waiting for.

Twitter: _kishajohnson
Instagram: kishajohnson and DearSisVlog
Tik Tok: AuthorLakisha and _DearSis
Email: authorlakisha@gmail.com

About the Author

Lakisha has been writing since 2012 and has penned over thirty novels, devotionals, and journals. You can find topics of faith, abuse, marriage, love, loss, grief, losing hope etc. on the pages of her many books.

In addition to being a self-published author, she's also a wife of 24 years, mother of 2, Grammie to one, Co-Pastor of Macedonia MB Church in Hollywood, MS; Sr. Business Analyst with FedEx, Devotional Blogger, and the product of a large family. She's a college graduate with 2 Associate Degrees in IT and a Bachelor of Science in Bible.

Lakisha writes from her heart and doesn't take the credit for what God does because if you were to strip away everything; you'd see Lakisha is simply a woman who boldly, unapologetically, and gladly loves and works for God.

Ask her and she'll tell you, "It's not just writing, its ministry."

Please check out the many other books available by visiting my Amazon Page. For upcoming contests and give-a-ways, I invite you to like my Facebook page, AuthorLakisha, join my reading group Twins Write 2 or follow https://authorlakishajohnson.com/. You can also join my newsletter by clicking HERE. I promise not to bombard you.

Also available

A Compilation of Christian Stories: Box Set

Shattered Vows Box Set

The Family that Lies

The Family that Lies: Merci Restored

Dear God: Hear My Prayer

The Pastor's Admin

2:32 AM: Losing My Faith in God

The Forgotten Wife

The Marriage Bed

Chased

Broken

When the Vows Break 1

When the Vows Break 2

When the Vows Break 3

Shattered

Shattered 2

Tense

Covet

Last Call

I'm Not Crazy

Infidelity

Another Chance

Behind Closed Doors

While I Slept

Wondah

Almost Destroyed 1

First Lady on Kindle Vella

Bible Chicks: Book 2

Doses of Devotion

You Only Live Once: Youth Devotional

HERoine Addict – Journal

Be A Fighter - Journal

Surviving Me - Journal

Made in the USA
Middletown, DE
28 March 2025

73390058R00167